To A

I hope you enjoy
them ☺

xx

APERITALES LETTER BITES

First edition: December 2020.
ISBN: 978-1-80049-161-8.
Publisher: Independent Publishing Network.
©: Text: Alba García Marcos.
©: Layout: Roma García.
©: Illustration: Ana Jarén.
©: Translation: Luis Andrés Peñaloza Rodríguez.
https: www.lasletrasdealba.es

To my grandpa. I hope you are proud of me wherever you are, eating your almonds and drinking your little glass of red wine. I'm sorry it took me so long to write this book.

PROLOGUE

The Flavors of my Life

I have a sweet tooth, but if I had to choose a flavor that defined my life, it would be a salty one; the pure salt flavor, and this never ceases to surprise me because almost all the dishes I prepare are quite tasteless.

But if I close my eyes to remember salty tastes, the first one that comes to my mind is that of salt water, every time a wave sent me tumbling and went through my nose and mouth. Also, the coarse salt of fresh fish and the sea bass in salt of any restaurant in Cadiz.

I remember other salty memories from my childhood, like the cheese puffs or the chorizo sandwiches I used to eat at recess. My grandma's mince soup. The popcorn at the cinema while watching Beauty and the Beast for the fourth time, or the macaroni with tomato.

After that, everything is candy and chocolate flavored. Like Ferrero Rocher chocolates, which indicated the beginning of Christmas, accompanied by coconut balls. The red jelly beans that I used to buy at the kiosk or the chocolate bars on Sundays while watching a movie. And, of course, those ice creams that melted in a few seconds during the summer (what a great discovery it was to realize that one could eat ice creams all year round).

Other flavors came late to my palate, like butter, croquettes or lentils. I suppose that you eventually rediscover them or admit that you don't know how you could have lived so long without them. And, when you admit that now you like what you used to hate, you'll want to try different dishes, cuisines and flavors; I call that maturing your taste.

And now that I'm in this search for out-of-the-ordinary restaurants and chefs who don't just do the usual in their kitchens, I also intend to give value again to the flavors that are stuck in your head and accompany you along the way. Like the spiciness of the stinky cheese top in the crappiest bar of your town, or the warmth of the glass of wine that you toast for no reason. Like the tastiness of fried food in a beach bar or the succulent grease of that bacon sandwich; the greasier, the better.

I miss them, all those flavors and the memories linked to them.

PASODOBLE «AND IT WAS MY GRANDMOTHER CHARI»

And it was my grandmother Chari
who raised her children
frying fish.
And it was your grandmother Angustias
who cooked the beans
that others have had dinner.
Your grandmother Rafaela
mashed the salmorejo
with oil and garlic
and with tomato and salt,
while in Almería
another old woman crumbled the bread,
and it was your grandmother
María del Mar.
Granny Sebastiana
stewed in Huelva
potatoes with cuttlefish,
breast-feeding ten children,
and her sacred milk wasn't enough,
wasn't enough,
wasn't enough.
And also,
remember,
how in Seville
cooked the stew

on her stove
your grandmother Esperanza
and, at the same time,
in her casserole she stewed the best pottage
of Málaga
your grandmother Paula,
and her house was her cage.
In the pots where time boils
gave the grandmothers
their sacred tendon
for hunger and sorrows,
with no other right
than their dignity.

Text by Miguel Ángel García Argüez

INDEX

PROLOGUE 7

PASODOBLE «AND IT WAS MY GRANDMOTHER CHARI» 9

INDEX... 11

   SOUR 15

      MY GRANDMOTHER'S BREAD 15

      THE LEMON IN MY THROAT.......................................17

      THE WINE OF MEMORIES 19

      AN ITCHING REVENGE 21

      THE FLYING PIGS 23

      THE NEW YORK DRAMA CAKE...................................25

      A MEATY PRANK 28

      THE PEKING DUCK OF FREEDOM 31

      THE PISTO OF HAPPINESS 33

      THE APPLES OF THE CASTLE 35

   SWEET 39

      THE GOOD-LUCK PINEAPPLE....................................39

      CHERRY BONBONS 41

      THE HONEY CAKE 43

      GRANNY'S JAM 45

THE LIFE-SAVING SANGRIA 47

SWEET ODE TO ALL THE SPICY 50

THE DULCE DE LECHE IS THE SIGN 52

THE SUGAR BALLOON 54

THE MAGIC ICE CREAM 56

THE SWEET WAIT 58

SALTY 61

THE SALT OF LIFE 61

THE FISH IN THE WAITING ROOM 63

THE CITY CIRCUS AND THE SUMMER OYSTERS 65

RIBS FOR THE HANGOVER 67

SEA MACKERELS 69

REFLECTIONS WITH A TASTE OF ESPETO 71

THE PARSNIP OF TRUTH 73

MY GRANDFATHER'S TURBOT 75

THE LOBSTER FROM THE PAST 77

CHARLIE'S TORTELLINI 79

SPICY 81

THE CHILI AND HIM 81

THE IMPROVISED MICHELADA 83

THE WINE OF DESIRE 86

PADRÓN PEPPERS PT. 1 88

PADRÓN PEPPERS PT. 2 90

THE CRUISE'S CACTUS SORBETS 93

PAKORA FOR DINNER...95

A TORTUROUS DESSERT 97

A RAVIOLI-SHAPED DECISION 99

THE ONION DANCE 101

BITTER..103

THE CANDY OF DEFEAT 103

THE TEA CEREMONY 106

THE BITTER ORANGE 109

THE SECRET IN THE BEARNAISE SAUCE 111

THE PLUM PIE 113

NIGHTMARE AT BREAKFAST 115

DARK CHOCOLATE 118

THE ANTS OF FREEDOM 120

ICE CREAM ON THE BEACH 122

THE BITTER TASTE OF MEMORIES 123

SAVORY OR UMAMI...127

THE EGGPLANT PAINTING..127

THE OKONOMIYAKIS AND THE KITCHEN IN OSAKA 129

THE HORSE MEAT AND HER......................................131

ADRIEN'S FIRST RATATOUILLE................................133

THE SOUP RITUAL 135

SALAD NUMBER 11..137

THE SECRET CRAB 139

THE PORTUGUESE TEMPURA...................................141

DUCK FEATHERS 143

THE FIRST FISH 145

ACKNOWLEDGMENTS 147

SOUR

MY GRANDMOTHER'S BREAD

It is said that the taste of bread depends on its ingredients, and I always wonder what those breads that taste like gum are made of. My grandfather always said that real bread tastes like my grandmother's bread. And that's a truth that no matter how many years go by. Even though she's gone, no one can argue with it, because I've never tasted the same kind again.

My grandmother's bread tasted like lactic acid, cereal and some kind of indescribable sourness. Like toasted crust. Like the humidity of her crumb. Like her clean hands soaked in the dough. Like the oil that dominated the table. Like the hot milk in my glass. Like tomatoes seasoned with garlic. Like her coffee kisses in the morning and the sweetness of her hugs.

And that unique flavor was slowly kneaded with the happy tune that always played on the radio at that hour and the sight of my grandfather lost between the pages of the newspaper, with his hoarse voice singing Neruda's Ode to Bread to bring a smile to my grandmother's face every morning.

She loved poetry and was devoted to her cooking. Perhaps that's why that ode was the perfect summary of her passions and the irrevocable sign to start having breakfast every morning in our little family of three.

«The kitchen was the excuse, but what was an excuse ended up being my passion».
Virgilio Martínez. CENTRAL

THE LEMON IN MY THROAT

"Wow! The recorder has run out of batteries. Well, I can still take notes. Just one last question, how did you become the Indiana Jones of cooking?"

"Are you sure you don't want us to stop and get you some new batteries?"

"No, thanks. I'm old-school, I know how to use a notebook and a pen. No problem."

"Okay, then. Somehow, I guess it all started the same day I broke my wrist. I've had many fractures in my life, but none hurt as much as the review I read that morning about my restaurant. I think everyone tried to hide it from me, noticing that all the copies were in the trash and those coteries that are formed when there is something to hide, but it was a futile attempt because, at that time, I was always avidly reading all the gastronomic publications. Many years have gone by, but I am still able to replicate that feeling of having swallowed a lemon whole and how, as I kept on reading, its sourness would seep into my guts. It wasn't what he said about my haughty attitude, or even about the lack of originality of my dishes. What hurt me the most was the truth hidden in his words about the lack of identity of my restaurant and how it somehow reflected all my insecurities. The end of the review was tragic; it described my restaurant as soulless. I guess now I have to thank for that sour pain I felt, since it made me wake up and want to tell a story that was never told. The story of a unique cuisine, of ancestral traditions and of a journey without return. And that's how that lemon in my throat turned me into the

17

Indiana Jones of cooking that I am now. Living among airplanes, mountains and pots and pans."

«After all, I can only cook one way. That's why each and every one of my projects carries my essence».
Eneko Atxa. AZURMENDI

THE WINE OF MEMORIES

Can a city get you drunk? That drunkenness that distracts your senses and covers everything with fog and colors. The same kind that can make you cry or convince you that you are the most powerful person in the world. Cities of light and shadow, contradictory and exciting. Yes, I think I'm drunk on London.

Every time I know I have to go to London, I get excited like a child on Christmas morning. I make plans for all the places I want to visit, even though I know I won't be able to make it, and refresh my English with podcasts that remind me of my limited language skills. I become like Joey from *Friends* when I visit all the tourist attractions in town. I even think about moving for a while. London absorbs me even before I set foot in one of its airports.

As I open the door of my hotel room, I think about this day and I get black-and-white flashbacks. The fatigue caused by the trip, the ride to the hotel, the cold shower, the neon lights of the buildings that the cab drove amongst to take me to the restaurant; the glitter of the dresses of the event's guests; the applause when someone uttered my name; the weight of the award and my acceptance speech. They were rewarding one of my wines, and I was traveling to the origin of this whole journey.

Exhausted and drunk from the night, I open a bottle of this very special wine and fly thousands of miles away. I feel the humidity of the grass on my feet and the scourge of the wind on my face. My mother and grandmother are peeling beans in the kitchen, and several pots in the fire smell of broths and cod. And the white wine on the table. It tasted like memories, whispering to me through its grapes: "Beware of the cities that can get you drunk".

«You need to be happy when you are making mole or tamales,
otherwise they won't come out right».
Daniela Soto-Innes. COSME

AN ITCHING REVENGE

Dear Diary:

Today I had an argument with that fool Susana in the school playground. Cristina, Marta, Rebeca and I were talking about the essay that teacher Rosalía had sent us this morning. We had to write about what we wanted to be when we grew up, and everyone was pretty clear about it, except for me.

Cristina wants to be an astronaut. I know she can do it, since she's the smartest one in the class and knows a lot about stars and planets. Marta dreams of being a doctor like her dad, which is why she is always taking care of us when we fall while racing or get an injury. And Rebeca plans to study to be a scientist, since she wants to discover many new things in a lab full of gadgets like the ones in our science class. But I don't know what to write in the essay because my friends say that I can only choose one thing, and I want to be many things. I would like to go to the Olympics with the swimming team, or the basketball team, or the track team, since I am always the first one to get to the finish line. But I also like cooking, and sometimes I win the contests that mom, grandma and I organize to see who prepares the best dish.

My friends were helping me decide, but Susana, who has always been a bit envious of me, arrived and said if I liked cooking, what I had to do was stay home and be a mom, as if you could only be one thing. And that's not true. You can be a mom and a chef, or a mom and a teacher, like teacher Rosalía, but she says that because she's not good at anything and losing bothers her. Susana is very prideful, so she never listens when we want to explain something to her.

So, after arguing with her and losing recess in the process, I told her that I was sure she would be a great mom someday, giving her one of the red candies that I made with my grandma last weekend. She took three more from the box because she thought they were strawberry, but they were filled with chili and itching powder. If she were a great cook like me, she would know.

Yes, I think I figured out what I will be when I grow up: the best chef in the world.

THE FLYING PIGS

The room where Colette is located is a huge room with white walls and high ceilings. Center of the room, there is a disproportionately large orange table full of scattered sheets of paper and colored pens. On a blue chair, she draws and writes scribbles that travel from her head to the paper while Indila's "Dernière Danse" plays over and over again. The rest is empty, lacking furniture and people who might interrupt her concentration.

The light enters slowly through the side windows, and a half-opened door reveals an unpolluted kitchen with a bouquet of tulips dominating the worktop.

It's dead quiet in the room, but Colette writes with her pen at high speed, cooking verses on those sheets of paper that taste like forests, recipes that sound like an orchestra, and ideas that are about to boil. Stories of different forms and poems of different flavors. Time flies whenever she creates something, and the only thing that can stop her is the roar of her gut. If she doesn't stop when her gut demands food, her head begins to spin, dreaming of flying pigs emerging from her hair.

She is hungry, but she decides to take a bath first. She drags her chair back to get up, as if she were a little girl, and walks almost mindlessly towards the bathroom. She doubts for a moment whether to go to the kitchen first, but her feet make the final decision, convincing her to ignore her inner voice. She prepares the bathtub with warm water and bubbles while she

23

undresses. The combination of hunger, sleep and ideas that still jump like frogs in her head begins to cause her hallucinations, like those pigs with daisies in their mouths, and some disturbing questions: Like what human flesh tastes like? She doesn't know how much time has passed, but her fingers are as wrinkled as raisins. She has never liked raisins, so she decides to get out of the bathtub. A foot slips, a hand doesn't touch the floor on time, and her head hits the edge of the tub. Suddenly, she sees her pigs carrying her to a floor full of pillows.

Some hours passed, but they seemed like days, and her only company were those animals flying in a sky so blue that it was dizzying and resembled the sea of San Sebastián. When she opened her eyes, she realized that life was too short to keep hiding her creations. Each line of those sheets of paper would be a dish, and each dish would be a poem that would fly up to her mouth, like her beloved pigs entangled in her hair.

«I like extremes. I live in extremes. I always have».
Daniel Humm. ELEVEN MADISON PARK

THE NEW YORK DRAMA CAKE

Films have created a very particular role for regular bartenders. They are expected to be silent, patient and, above all, good listeners. Oh, and they also should be good advisors. However, the cinema and the real world seem to forget about the waiters who work in luxury restaurants. Everyone thinks we are statues that move like a military parade to serve the expensive dishes of a fancy menu. A repetitive and monotonous job, right? After all, what else could happen in a restaurant where everyone knows how to behave and no one ever gets drunk? At most, we end up blowing out birthday candles, celebrating anniversaries and dealing with occasional and hand requests, right? Let me tell you how wrong you are. What happened the other night was really bad.

Everything was set for the first shift of the night. The tables were spotless, the kitchen was ready and everyone was at their posts. We opened at eight, and the first reservation of the night arrived exactly a minute later. It was a table for four regular customers, so we knew them quite well. Besides, our pastry chef was a close friend of one of them.

They were two couples of old friends who had known each other since college. They had lived all kinds of adventures together until they became adults, living and working in the Big Apple. Sarah and Peter got married right out of college, and Susan and Paul did the same two years later. They lived in apartments in the same building and all of them had serious and important jobs.

But anyway, getting back to the story, the four of them sat at their usual table, next to one of the windows, after greeting the chef, who was also at restaurant that night. We didn't have any special events scheduled, which meant they had nothing to celebrate. If you were near the table, you could hear the typical conversations about how the week had gone while drinking a glass of wine and reading the menu suggestions.

That's when I approached them to explain that that night we had a special menu, including the chef's new creation. I spent fifteen minutes straight explaining to them how delicious the new dish was, its beauty, its uniqueness and the story behind it. Not even the best of the dramatic monologues could compete with my gastronomic recital.

The girls didn't believe that the main dish was a celery root with two balls, one of truffle, the other of mashed potatoes, but Peter convinced them right away and they grew interested in the special menu.

Everything went well until Sarah threw up the main course in front of everyone. The poor woman didn't manage to get out on time, and her friends and neighboring customers had to watch the celery turn to mush. A joy for the senses. After apologizing a thousand times, Sarah dropped the first bomb of the night and announced that she was pregnant. It was a surprise for her friends, but the one who should have been happiest. The future father had an unhappy face that didn't exactly fit the situation. Perhaps it was the fact of finding out so suddenly instead of in the privacy of their home, but Sarah was that spontaneous. She didn't know how to keep secrets from her best friends who, of course, were going to be the godparents.

They kept dining, but Peter's face didn't get any better. Sarah began to feel ill while Paul made an endless list of names for the baby. On the other hand, Susan got up to go say hello to our pastry chef in the kitchen. I was going in and out with the dishes, but at that moment I accompanied Susan to the kitchen and stayed there. What I heard between whispers, after an endless and friendly hug, left me perplexed.

Susan started to cry, and Megan, our pastry chef, took her to a corner to comfort her. I thought for a moment that those were tears of happiness, but when Susan confessed that she had been sleeping with Peter for months, I immediately understood the face of the future father. Apparently, they were going to confess the infidelity to their respective partners at the same time in the restaurant, but the announcement had shocked them. Also, she told Megan that Peter had secretly sent her a text message that said: "Change of plans. Mission aborted." How about that?

The unfaithful woman wiped away her tears and regained her composure for what was an Oscar-worthy performance. Later, I brought them a cake improvised by Megan and everyone pretended to be the happiest in the world. Half an hour later, they left and Megan decided to name her new cake "New York Drama."

So don't tell me that my job is boring or stuffy. With everything that goes on in this restaurant, I should become a Hollywood screenwriter!

«I spent many years thinking about how to make incredible dishes for an audience that represents 5% of the population. That's selfish».
Jefferson Rueda. A CASA DO PORCO

A MEATY PRANK

Rafa had been pulling pranks on her all her childhood. She couldn't remember a day when her brother wasn't the mastermind behind a lost toy, a broken vase or a sugar bowl full of salt. That was his way. He was the king of pranks and mischief, and she adored him despite all the tears she had shed because of him and the tantrums he had caused.

Then came the teenage years and the girls, and Rafa began to forget about teasing his little sister, even though he always saved something for big occasions, such as Christmas or family vacations. She still remembered that time when he made their parents believe that she was pregnant, and they fell for it because she had gained some weight that year. It was a short but intense drama.

Macarena kept reminiscing about all her brother's jokes while waiting for him at a table with a glass of wine. Thank God the jokes eventually stopped, even though she missed them at times. Well, in fact, she missed him. Since she decided to have her own business, she had only seen him a handful of times a year, always exhausted but happy. This time the excuse was that Rafa had to tell her something important, but the last few times he had told her the same thing, it always ended up being one of his pranks. So, she wasn't going to believe anything this time.

Her brother had asked her not to order anything from the menu because he wanted to surprise her. Rafa and his silly things. However, she was amused not knowing what she was going to eat, and finally her little brother had accepted that his dear sister was now a vegetarian. Rafa arrived, as usual, with dark circles under his eyes and radiating a charm that had always accompanied him from his birth. He was one of those people that always got what he wanted, and everyone loved him. He gave her a kiss on the cheek and began to ask for dishes at once, claiming that he was starving. Everything sounded wonderful: Tartar made of jelly, mushrooms, veggie sushi, noris... Lately, Japanese cuisine had become very popular in the city.

They devoured everything as they caught up with each other, although she had always preferred to listen to his endless anecdotes, like when they were kids and he would tell her made-up stories before going to bed. As always, time flew by, and when it was time for dessert, they ordered churros with chocolate and coffee. Rafa had a suspicious smile, so she decided to ask him about the important thing he wanted to tell her. He took his little sister's hand and, with a serious voice, told her: "Don't get mad, but everything you just ate is pork in different shapes, textures and flavors."

At that moment, Macarena didn't know whether to kill him or go to the bathroom and throw up. Nevertheless, she had to admit that that terrible prank had tasted great.

She doubted for a few seconds whether to tell him that she also had something important to say, but she decided to play the offended one, slapping him so that he would think she was furious with him. The slap felt harder than she intended, but in reality it was life that she was furious with; it was literally slipping through her fingers. It was like a macabre prank of fate.

*«I realized that if you listen to every customer, you'll go crazy
because it's always really subjective».*
Tim Raue. TIM RAUE

THE PEKING DUCK OF FREEDOM

Once upon a time there was a country known as *Übelnehmerisch* where one had to be very careful about what was said and how it was said to avoid offending the people. To avoid having the offended ones jump out of their beds with banners and kitchen knives to chase the person who talked too much.

Übelnehmerisch was controlled by a group of slant-eyed sages who dictated all the rules of behavior necessary to maintain the peace in the territory. Everything was described in a huge book, from how to get out of bed to the conversations that could be held in a public meeting. It was forbidden to speak using masculine pronouns to ensure that no woman would be offended; it was forbidden to talk about animals in general to ensure that the defenders of nature would not be offended; and, of course, it was forbidden to talk about politics or religion, since those were considered topics of great danger. The list was endless because every day there was at least one forbidden topic to add to the book.

One day, a very clever woman, who had been traveling around the world, arrived in this country. She quickly realized that if she wanted to survive, she would have to find a way to deceive the offended people of this land. Her street boxing skills would be of little use to her because everyone seemed happy, even though they could not talk about much.

She began to invent a new language with secret codes that only those rebels who, like her, wanted to talk about whatever they pleased, could understand. However, some snitches got out of hand and she almost ended up on the electric guillotine.

She remained hidden for a while until they forgot about her, and then, like a phoenix, she reemerged as a chef. It was in the kitchen where she found a way to survive and express her rebelliousness. If you couldn't talk about men, she hired as many as she could. If only Rubinstein was allowed to be heard, she would work listening to jazz, and if animals couldn't be eaten, she prepared a Peking duck that everyone devoured thinking it was fried seaweed. And that's how, in her kitchen, she got the freedom that the offended people wanted to take away from her. And they lived happily ever after... eating partridges (or Peking ducks).

«Chefs need to have their own identity and know exactly what they are doing. They should use ideas but never copy».
Peter Goossens. HOF VAN CLEVE

THE PISTO OF HAPPINESS

In this time of depressions and PowerPoint presentations, she had decided to give one last chance to those modern gurus who ensured your happiness by following their lists of definitive steps. They all claimed to have the key to success, but she quickly discovered that such teachings, adapted to the 21st century, were already in a number of older books.

She was wearing her incognito uniform: a very long coat and sunglasses, although she didn't know why, since not a single ray of sunshine ever came out in that grayish city. She decided to go on foot, even though the watch her brother had given her indicated a fifty-minute walk. However, she thought that in that timeframe she could prepare her mind for what she was going to hear. After an endless walk, there she was, half suffocated, in the last row of a cold and dark conference room akin to those situated in the many hotels of the city.

The on-duty guru began his talk on how to achieve happiness and she was about to space out and think about a thousand things at once. The truth was that meditation and the Zen state of mind had never been her thing. Even as a child, she surely had that hyperactivity disorder, but back then those things were solved by enrolling herself in a thousand extracurricular classes so that she could release her energy. The room was full, but she could still hear her guts growling. Now she was not only bored, but hungry as well.

She came back to reality just as the famous psychologist was asking the attendees what happiness meant for them. There were many similar answers, all very deep and emotional, and suddenly she knew the answer. A great revelation. It was very clear that happiness was finding a damn place where you can eat a decent ratatouille.

«I like to use regional ingredients that I have eaten from young and put in a lot of work to make them sparkle».
Andreas Caminada. SCHLOSS SCHAUENSTEIN

THE APPLES OF THE CASTLE

Once upon a time, there was a haunted castle that was hidden among some very high mountains. The people of the small village never wanted to go there because everyone who entered never returned home. So, the elders told stories of a castle haunted by ghosts. However, Pedro, one of the young shepherds, was very brave; he did not believe in ghosts, and much less in the one they said lived in that castle.

One day, Pedro left the sheep with his friend Luis and headed off to find the castle that everyone was talking about. It took him seven days to find it because there was a long railroad and the top of the mountain was steeped in clouds, covered in a snow that stifled the view. In the end, he found a huge door guarded by a very fat man who demanded that he left all his belongings outside as a requirement to enter. He did so, thinking that it hadn't been so difficult to get into the castle after all. No dragons, no impossible tests, just a guard with a poor security system.

As he entered, he gazed in awe all the details of the entrance. The impressive spiral staircase, the crystal chandeliers, the paintings similar to those he had once seen in the museum of the capital. Everything was spectacular. He was absorbed for a long time until he heard the noise of frying pans, shouts, chains and deeply depressing classical music in the background. When he arrived at what seemed to be the kitchen, his eyes couldn't believe it: many people dressed in white were obeying the orders of a very peculiar ghost. A mixture between his grandmother and Aladdin's genie, with radioactive green eyes, that screamed and insulted the people hypnotized by such fiery gaze. When they finished obeying the orders, everyone prepared a mile-long table with dishes of all colors and flavors. Those combinations were so unusual that they only made the ghost angrier, who would throw the food into the air after tasting it. The ghost kept shouting the same thing: "Nothing. They taste like nothing. Go back to the kitchen and do it again!" And so the slaves spent all day and all night cooking for the ghost.

After seeing that horror show, Pedro decided to rescue all those villagers who had disappeared over the years. He snuck into the kitchen and took advantage of the fact that the ghost had gone to nap and cry over all the wasted food. In the kitchen, he talked to one of the slaves, a young boy who had been under the influence of the ghost for only a few months and still remembered why it had them there. After listening to him, Pedro learned the ghost's story. She was once a grandmother who died of poisoning and swore revenge on the whole village, which had been her home. As part of her revenge, she hypnotized everyone who dared to enter the castle and forced them to cook non-stop until they created a dish that tasted amazing, since the poison destroyed her tastebuds.

After listening to the story, Pedro got down to business and started cooking. First, he went into the garden to pick several apples, as he assumed that, in order to create something different, he shouldn't use the strange ingredients he had seen in the kitchen. When he washed them, he began to cook them secretly for several days, helped by the boy to prevent the ghost from finding him. After a week, the apples had been turned into sweets, liqueurs, wine, ice cream and vinaigrettes; Pedro prepared a small table for the ghost to enjoy.

When the ghost arrived and found that table at the main entrance, Pedro's legs trembled, but Raimunda, the ghost, didn't scream or cast any spell on him with her green gaze. Instead, she was curious about the simplicity of the dishes, taking one to taste it right away. Her eyes grew big as a child's, changed color and, little by little, as she tasted the wine and sweets, all the scary features disappeared until she turned into an adorable grandmother, who, with tears in her eyes, whispered: "My tongue tastes like afternoons in the countryside. Like my mother's songs when she used to make compote, like the village's summer fair, like my first love. My tongue has recovered the flavors of my memory."

And that's how Peter freed the ghost of her nightmare and the slaves of the spell. The castle was turned into a grand restaurant, where Pedro welcomed with open arms all those who wanted to revisit their childhood through his dishes and apples.

Snip, snap, snout, this delicious tale's told out.

SWEET

«For me, a gourmet 20-course menu has no more value than a roast chicken in some backyard in Macedonia, or some tacos al pastor in the streets of Mexico».
Rene Redzepi. NOMA

THE GOOD-LUCK PINEAPPLE

When Ali closed the door and said goodbye with a big smile, I knew that the door wasn't the only thing closing. We were all aware that this was the end of a period of plans, dreams and castles in the air.Which, with that slamming of the door, had become reality.

In front of me, I had fifty-seven boxes to unpack and a lot to do, but moving always made me hungry. I thought I still had time to cook something fast if I could find the most basic utensils and the bag with food in it.

My family had agreed to give me a couple of days off to start putting things in order, especially my ideas, but we all knew that they were actually giving me space to organize my own chaos, trying not to interfere with the map I had drawn in my head. Honestly, I have no idea what I would do without them.

It seemed that all the appliances were working. So, while I lit the fire, I put on the counter the ingredients that Ali had prepared for me: bread, salt, pepper, eggs, salmon, oil, vinegar and wine. There wasn't much choice, but the option of toast with poached eggs was simply irresistible.

All my senses were focused on that huge kitchen, which was now naked and welcoming me with such a humble dish. My head kept bouncing back and forth between the mountain of untidy boxes and the endless list of things to do. Those boxes contained everything I didn't want to leave behind, but I needed a sign that told me I was on the right track. I guess insecurities always creep in when moving so that you continue to be filled with doubts.

Just as I was taking the eggs out, I noticed that there was something on the kitchen floor. I bent down to pick it up and then I saw it. There, hidden in a corner, was a small pineapple. It wasn't like the ones we had in the restaurant; it was wilder, as if it had slipped into my kitchen in an attempt to elude its written destiny. I kept watching it for a long time and ended up putting it in my pocket before finishing what would be my brunch. I smiled. That was the sign I was looking for.

«How to make a dish that reflects the passage of time? We need to make edible poetry».
Andoni Luis Aduñiz. MUGARITZ

CHERRY BONBONS

All three of us remember and recount the day of the fire differently. Elena remembers it full of sadness, with that existential melancholy that always accompanies her everywhere. Eduardo always dyes everything red when he remembers it, like the filling of his bonbons and the flames of the fire. And I, ironically, am the one who can break down the moments and revive the hopes of that day.

That morning, the three of us woke up very early for different reasons. Elena wanted to finish correcting her students' philosophy papers. By then, everything should have been more than finished, but she always gave her underperforming students an extra opportunity to start the year off right through some fascinating work in which they had to question fundamental aspects of life. She called that work *bites of the soul*, and it was her way of revolutionizing an educational system in which she had stopped believing long ago.

I remember the cold rays of sunshine sneaking through the window and getting tangled up in her black, messy hair, and how Elena would drink her third cup of coffee at her desk while reading aloud some of her students' most interesting paragraphs. Neither Eduardo nor I paid much attention to her, except when she began to laugh out loud, forcing us to ask her to explain the nonsense of those hidden geniuses.

It was around ten o'clock in the morning and Eduardo had already spent more than four hours in the kitchen experimenting with the dishes he wanted to prepare that year for Christmas Eve. We were three hermits who, due to life's circumstances, had formed this small improvised family. Although none of us really liked those dates, Eduardo always forced us to comply with certain culinary traditions, such as his copious dinners on December 24th. His dishes were anything but traditional, but it was his excuse to spend days in the kitchen breaking the rules as his particular form of revolution.

The only tradition I kept up every year was to listen to the Christmas Lottery Draw on the radio on December 22nd. It was like a siren's song that hypnotized me for hours and heightened all my senses. Perhaps that was why, that morning, I could smell the cherry liqueur from the bonbons that Eduardo was eating in the kitchen, the coffee from Elena's cups, the Italian incense that burned in the living room... I was also the first one to smell the smoke from the flames that suddenly appeared in the kitchen after Eduardo left for a few minutes without telling us. Afterwards, everything was a chaos that lasted several minutes; there were screams, frantic running, unexpected kisses and mistakes that made the fire which ended up ruining our kitchen bigger

That day of black walls and red bonbons changed everyone's life. Elena lost the philosophical meditations of her students and ended up giving them all a good grade as a utopian Christmas present, after taking a leave of absence due to depression. I, on the other hand, finally managed to fulfill my desire when I tasted those cherry bonbons on Eduardo's creamy lips.

*«We're cooking in modern style, but when you close your eyes,
it's like eating your grandma's cooking».*
Vladimir Mukhin. WHITE RABBIT

THE HONEY CAKE

I should be given some money for my services to this community. And I'm not talking about the dishes I prepare for the neighbors, I'm happy to do that, because what else would I be doing with those skinny students on the fifth floor who only eat snacks and junk food? Or with my neighbor across the street. Even though she's a year younger than me, she doesn't have the sight or the skills to do the cooking anymore?

I'm talking about safety. Some people mistake my visual and auditory skills for cheap gossip, but if you got it, flaunt it. My past as a former spy is still with me. The peephole in my door is my treasure and, fortunately or unfortunately, depending on who you ask, the walls are made of paper.

My condition as a grandmother helps me to get everyone to forgive my hobbies, like opening the door right away if I see through the peephole that there are more than two people talking on the landing, or spending several hours leaning out of my small balcony with a red notebook and a pencil.

At first, I guess I was doing it for professional deformation and to kill time, but since the neighbor on the second floor settled in, everything started to smell fishy to me.

The new neighbor's name is Yuri, and he says he's Russian, the purest Russian. One-hundred-percent Russian blood in his veins. Or so he says, anyway. However, when I see this five-foot-four man with long jet-black hair and no tattoos on his arms, he doesn't look very Russian to me. Besides, he has a perfect accent; one of those that you can't guess the region, and his house is utterly silent. I never see him at the bar where men meet to drink vodka in the afternoon, and he's only at home to sleep, especially on Mondays.

That's why Mondays have become my favorite day of the week. It's the only day I can hear his steps and if I try a little harder, some of his few phone conversations. But what I like most about Mondays are the smells coming from his apartment. He leaves very early in the morning to go to the market and when he returns, I always try to be at the doorway to have brief conversations with him. They're almost always about cooking since Yuri says he's a cook.But if it's true, he's a very unusual cook. Sometimes I can't even describe the smells that come from his apartment, and when I look at the bags he brings from the market, there are ingredients that are not very Russian.

He is always very polite in answering my questions, and so, little by little, I have been writing down in my red notebook everything I have been able to find out about him. Little details. Like when he told me that his favorite dessert was honey cake, since it reminded him of his *babushka*. The truth is always in the small details.

Today is Monday, and I've been preparing a honey cake all morning. I'm thinking of giving it to Yuri as an excuse to get into his apartment. Maybe I'll put a microphone in it. I doubt I will find out the whole truth while he eats the cake, but at least I'll be able to try one of those strange things he cooks and check if he really is a cook.

«I believe that Human Beings are the heart of Odette, and it is important that we put them at the center of the creative process».
Julien Royer. ODETTE

GRANNY'S JAM

I go to see her every morning before work. It's our routine, and I've never missed it since she started to leave the house. At first, we had regular conversations and she would ask me about my job, family or any of the news I had seen on TV the night before. Then, she stopped talking and just wanted me to come and see her to read her her favorite stories, the ones her father used to read to her when she was little. She once said that it was the only time of the day when she was truly happy, traveling back to her childhood through stories of pirates and princesses.

Today I overslept, and in my haste I forgot to take something from the bookshelf to read to her. When I arrive at her house, there she is, sitting at the table and smearing some jam on the freshly toasted rolls she has just made. I know the stories by heart at this point, so, when I see that lovely scene, I approach her to kiss her white hair and start telling her a story that begins one spring morning.

The woman in our story has finished peeling and washing the red berries. Her kitchen smells of orchard and sugar, and there's a little man helping her put all those fruits into a big pot to cook them. As they wait for the fruit to boil, she answers the thousand questions the boy asks her, prepares him some hot milk and tells him to keep an eye on the jar of sugar that will be poured into the pot in a while. The child drinks his glass of milk and brings a stool closer to the fire so that he can properly pour the sugar and lemon juice under her supervision. Together, they stir the mixture with a wooden spoon and count the minutes to monitor the boiling time. He feels important for what he is doing, and she looks at him with pride.

Only she knows when to remove the pot from the heat to let it cool down. It's a secret she'll tell him someday to make the jam so delicious. Finally, the two of them pour the jam into small glass jars and close them with red ribbons. He still needs some practice, but his grandmother assures him that he will eventually do it even better than she does.

The boy knows that is impossible, but pretends to believe her. There is no one in the world who could make jam like his grandmother. Even now that the woman is locked in her memories, she smiles as she listens to the story and promises the man next to her that tomorrow they will make jam together again.

«My family loves the fact that I grew up to be a chef because I was a very picky eater as a child, and quite awkward».
James Lowe. LYLE´S

THE LIFE-SAVING SANGRIA

Let me give you some advice: don't ever host a dinner party at your house if you live in a foreign country, in a tiny apartment, and don't know how to cook. I'm being serious. Don't even try it. Don't get carried away just because you have something to celebrate, have a special guest or want to show your foreign friends that your country's food is the best in the world. That's why restaurants exist. And if you don't trust me, I'll tell you everything that can go wrong.

You're in a bar drinking a beer with your friends from the office and suddenly the conversation shifts to Mary's trip around Andalusia and how well she ate there. You don't know a damn thing about cooking, but, come on, if they're talking about the food of your country, you have every right to be an authority on the subject and list all the dishes that are a must if one goes to the south of Spain. The beers are doing their thing, and the gazpacho with the Valencian paella and the tapas with Basque skewers are beginning to get mixed up. Next thing you know, you get up to propose a toast and invite everyone to come to your house for dinner next week.

Don't panic, three friends having some tapas is not a big deal. However, without knowing how, the three English friends turn into ten, and you find yourself looking for a table and folding chairs at Amazon to accommodate them all in eight square meters. You haven't even started to make a shopping list yet and you know that dinner is going to cost you an arm and a leg.

Now let's move on to the menu. After convincing them that paella is not eaten at night and that there will be sangria, you think of a tapas dinner and some portions, as if they were at El Pimpi or Columela's Tapería. You write down the basics: bread for the sandwiches, some good ham, Manchego cheese, tomatoes to make salmorejo, shrimps, squid, etc. When you finish, you realize you need to start crossing things off your list because it is something informal, not the banquet of the Last Supper.

With the menu already decided, it's time to go shopping. As you've always hated traditional markets and you don't intend to get up early on the weekend, you have no choice but to go to a supermarket. And here begins the nightmare: the bread is anything but bread; if you really want some ham, you have to at the very least sell a kidney; the fish is all frozen and you want to cry when you get to the seafood aisle. However, you quickly remember that you are wearing Morrison shoes on a Saturday morning, so you can't afford to make a scene. Besides, your friends have only been to Spain once in their lives, so it won't be too hard to impress them.

In the middle of this crisis, you think of buying some British meat and sight a duck on sale. You quickly look for a recipe on your phone and, after a moment, you freeze. Where exactly are you going? You haven't eaten duck your whole life, except for pâté! Now dinner has become a Hispanic-British mix, but you head for your mini-apartment to spend the rest of the day in the kitchen anyway.

You put on some music in Spotify, put on some comfortable clothes and start the dinner ritual. You wash all the ingredients, organize them by dishes, write down the recipes on post-its and stick them on the containers, and pour yourself a glass of sweet wine to get inspired. The duck is still defrosting, the oven stops working and you just realize that you don't have enough cutlery and glasses for everyone. With each setback, you drink another glass of Canasta to drown your worries.

You don't even know how many hours have gone by, but your time has come to a head. When the first guests arrive, you receive them with a table without a tablecloth, since you had also forgotten to buy it, full of bread and two burnt potato omelets. Luckily, there is so much sangria that you hope that soon nobody will know the difference between an anchovy and a sardine.

«The ego is like cholesterol, there is a good and a bad one».
Dabiz Muñoz. DIVERXO

SWEET ODE TO ALL THE SPICY

I know why you demand their tears
by lighting flames in their tongues.

You like to feel powerful,
taking revenge on all those who do not understand you,
challenging them in bets to see who is the bravest.

You hide like a child playing hide-and-seek,
under different shapes and colors;
but everyone sees you as a raging dragon,
and you, feeling helpless,
flap your wings on their taste buds
until they beg for mercy on their knees,
dying of thirst.

I, however, perceived you beyond the fire
and fell in love with your warmth, your nuances.

Do not envy the sweetness of the candies,
for it is sticky and cloying,
a cheap magic trick that numbs the senses.

Be proud of your body,
of your essence,
It is they who do not know how to handle your onslaught.

If they knew how to taste you properly
and dance among your waves,

they would discover how sweet you are underneath your
rebelliousness.

You can camouflage yourself in ice cream,
lollipops and cakes,
in pies, muffins and chocolates;
you can surprise from the first bite,
like a boy who steals your first kiss,
like an unexpected gift,
like a life-changing stroke of fate.

One must take it slowly to gain your trust,
as the wild animal you want to eat from your hand
in sips,
with a shy tongue full of respect and excitement,
without stupid boldness or macho bets.

When you realize that you are in front of a mouth like this,
you are a gentleman full of gallantry;
you don't explode suddenly, you don't kick, you don't scream,
you stop at foreplay,
wetting the cave with saliva,
and you wait patiently for them to get used to you and ask for
more.
Then, that mouth repeats,
gets addicted to your damn bursts
and never leaves you.
Not even for all the candy in the world.

«Gastronomy is about affection, not about ego».
Pablo Jesús Rivero. DON JULIO

THE DULCE DE LECHE IS THE SIGN

We had seen *Friends* a zillion times, and for days I had been feeling like Mike when he decided to propose to Phoebe. I had imagined the scene a thousand times in my head, in a thousand different ways, and in some cases she even said no. I guess my imagination suffers from stage fright as well. Once I had dismissed all the options that involved selling my organs, I chose a more traditional approach: an intimate dinner, with her favorite bottle of wine. Same as Chandler's initial plan, although I hoped that no unwelcome person would appear theatrically.

She's not very romantic, definitely not the type of girl who has always dreamed of getting married and starting a family, but I guess deep down we all want to feel special. We met one day during a torrential downpour, and that same day we ended up under a fireplace drying our bodies with the heat of the fire. Since then, that element has always been very special in our relationship.

She is a wine lover, so I thought that asking her the big question in a restaurant where the fire was the protagonist, and her favorite wine the sidekick, was a winning combination.

The only thing left was to find the right moment. I didn't think it was wise to put the ring inside a dish, since every half second I needed to know that I had it on me to reassure myself. Luckily, she is so absent-minded that she wouldn't notice my nervousness at all.

The occasion was an anniversary surprise, so she chose a breathtaking dress that caught everyone's attention. When we entered, her face lit up with a lovely smile because we had reached "that place where the fire embraces you and time stands still."

Dinner ended so fast, and we ate empanadas, sweetbreads, and hors d'oeuvres that melted in our mouths. It ended so fast that I had few options left for the big moment, and the dulce de leche dessert we had just ordered was a sign that I had to decide soon. When she was distracted watching the grill man play with the fire, I took a pen out of my jacket and wrote on the sticker of the bottle: "Life is too short to drink bad wines, do you want to drink the good ones with me?" For someone who didn't drink alcohol like me, that was quite a statement of intent.

She turned around just as I finished putting the pen back in my jacket, and I almost dropped the bottle on the floor out of fright. Luckily, she grabbed it in time to avoid disaster.

When she went to take the first bite of the dessert, she saw the sticker and said, "Let's always drink life as if we are going to die of thirst." And that answer got me drunk with pure happiness.

«I got D minuses in chemistry and all of the sciences, and now I'm known as a molecular gastronomist».
Grant Achatz. ALINEA

THE SUGAR BALLOON

I remember that morning for its cold weather; it was colder than any winter morning in Chicago. I was torn between indulging in a few more hours of sleep or doing something productive, but I ended up getting out of bed only to wander around the house. It was one of those days when laziness became a part of my mood, but I took a shower by inertia and went to make myself some breakfast.

While I was looking for something among the leftovers to challenge my morning creativity, I tried to remember the flavors I had learned yesterday. I should have continued with the practice, but none of those flavors came to mind and I didn't want to get frustrated on my day off. In the end, I prepared a sesame bagel with cream cheese, tomato, salt and pepper. Then, I decided it was best to take a walk around the city despite the cold weather.

The house was quite messy, and so was my closet. I remember thinking that it was the perfect analog of my own mind, full of chaotic memories and ideas scattered everywhere. I smelled the oak wood of the closet and traveled for a few seconds to Michigan, to my childhood, suddenly feeling a strong need for sweet food in my system.

Sometimes these things would happen to me, a taste would slip into my memories and stay with me all day until it became an obsession, like bubbles in champagne or salt stuck in fish scales.

Now I could only think of cotton candy, caramelized apples and chocolate fountains, as if I had been trapped in my childhood.

My whole body kept demanding sugar, so I finished dressing, grabbed the scarf that was lying on the couch and closed the door. I put the keys in my left hand, since I hate to carry things in my pockets, and wandered around the streets of Chicago. The humidity began to seep into my bones, but I kept thinking about candy and sweets, and at that moment, I was sure that those memories wouldn't leave me until I ate something or invented a new creation. This was happening just when I needed a new dessert for the menu.

I passed by the history museum and the zoo until I reached Lincoln Park, where I came across a boy holding his grandfather's hand and a balloon bigger than him. I knew tragedy was coming when the helium balloon slipped out of his grip and disbelief soon turned into a fountain of tears. I wanted to buy him another one, but I didn't have any cash in my pockets. Then, as revelation drew over me, I ran to the restaurant.

That was the morning I created a sugar balloon for all the children who had lost theirs due to a gust of wind.

«After all, when you cook and serve with your heart and soul,
from your true feelings, everything is special».
Jonnie Boer. DE LIBRIJE

THE MAGIC ICE CREAM

Today we were asked at school what our parents do. They are always very nice to me when they talk about our parents because they know I no longer have a mother. However, when I spoke about my father's job, they all started to laugh. But I didn't tell a joke.

My dad is a magician; he makes things appear that didn't exist before. Okay, he doesn't use a wand nor do things appear in a black hat, but he uses his hands and magic. Maybe they laughed because they don't believe me. There are always some kids who are jealous in my class. The wizard Merlin had his book of magic, and my father has one too, which he reads when he needs to know how to do something. Maybe Mom was a witch, since witches make magic potions and use fire, just like she did. I don't know about Mom, but what I said about Dad is true.

One day, we went to the countryside to pick up strawberries, the next we had jam at home. The other day, from the tomatoes we had in the garden, he made a sauce for my macaroni. With the fruits that Grandma brings, he always makes juices and mixes the flour, water and salt in the bread that we have for breakfast on the weekends.

Mrs. Lucia explained to us that this kind of magic belongs to cooks, who can create very tasty food with a few ingredients. I know she never lies, but that thing my dad does is called magic, so I sat in my chair and never spoke again all day.

When I got home, I waited for my dad to arrive to talk to him seriously and tell him what had happened in class. And he said to me:

"Teresa, there are many kinds of magicians with different names, and mine is the one Lucia told you about. But not everyone knows that we, cooks, do magic, and some people call it cooking. But you know the truth, and you have seen what happens in the kitchen. Besides, I'm going to tell you a secret and you'll see what magic can do: Dad is going to turn a prison into a wonderful restaurant, but you can't tell anyone about it."

Listening to Dad made me happy because I like it when he tells me secrets, and he always tells the truth. And, of course, because he did my favorite trick and made the yogurt that I don't like disappear from my favorite ice cream.

«Modern cuisine is about cooks and not so much about territories. We invent new worlds».
Joan Roca. CELLER CAN ROCA

THE SWEET WAIT

As I buckle up and try to find the least uncomfortable position for the two-hour flight ahead, I think about how fast everything has happened. A whole year of waiting that will disappear in a few days. It seems like a lie.

I still remember the jumps of joy in the middle of the darkness when we were finally able to put a date on it. Although crying is always my first reaction, I literally jumped up and down and screamed in silence, hoping that the neighbors wouldn't wake up. It was a rare mix of surprise, triumph and love, because who does such a crazy thing if not for love?

And even though the best is yet to come, the waiting has been part of the process. Like cooking on a slow fire. We've been preparing all the details for the big day together, which meant looking for the perfect place, the dress, the savings, organizing the trip and so on. If it was going to be a once-in-a-lifetime experience, it had to be organized in a big way.

Many times I was told that I was going too far, that it was no big deal and that it wasn't even worth all the effort. I know, my people are not very empathetic or romantic, and I am not one to follow advice. So, here we are, coming to a lost land that will nourish my soul.

If 365 days have flown by, these last hours have been shooting stars. Wearing my best dress and a nervous stomach, I squeeze his hand, get out of the car and take a breath to enjoy a night in the best restaurant in the world. There are waits that are worthwhile.

SALTY

«I talk only to the grill; it's the only one who understands me».
Víctor Arguinzoniz. ASADOR ETXEBARRI

THE SALT OF LIFE

We are not even ten people holding a vigil for my grandmother in her cold stone house, and half of them are townspeople. Our family has not been able to come because it was such an unexpected death and, let's admit it, nobody ever wants to come to this town that is lost in the middle of nowhere. The road is horrible, it's always cold and there's no mobile signal.

The silence is sepulchral, except for a few cries, and in my head there is only an intermittent idea that gets bigger and bigger. Maybe it's my habit of going against the world or just the peace I feel right now, but I have just decided to accept the mayor's proposal to come and live in this desert. The city is overrated, and my grandmother always said it: New year, new life.

It can't be that difficult to live at a different pace. There is even a new trend: People deciding to stop using social networks and live completely unconnected. Why shouldn't I be one of those people? If, in fact, everything is smoke and mirrors: The trends of meditation, yoga and even slow cooking ... Come on! I want to cook and eat like my grandmother used to, without looking at the clock, because knowing when something is cooked is a matter of looking, practicing and a lot of patience.

Everyone has already left, leaving the fire on to heat the house. I don't know if it is the right decision, but my gut tells me that I should honor her by going to the town bar and eating a good grilled steak.

There are wounds that burn even without salt, but she knew how to heal them with pampering and patience, the same way she used to cook.

«We do have that creative ego and we want to do new things.
But we have internalized it».
Oriol Castro. ENJOY (DISFRUTAR)

THE FISH IN THE WAITING ROOM

I've always hated waiting rooms. They are like black holes that engulf you, where time stands still and one must remain silent. Nowadays everyone seems to have something to do with their cell phones, and even waiting rooms become a breath of fresh air that allows you to catch up on all the things pending.

However, back in the day, for a ten-year-old boy who had to sit in a dentist's waiting room, the world came to a standstill and boredom was the main character.

My mother always told me to take a book, but I always forgot about it. At first it was unintentional, and then it was because they hung a new painting in the dentist's reception area. Which quickly became the center of attention of my weekly visits.

The first time I saw it, it didn't seem much to me. It was a typical seafaring scene, where two fishermen were beside their boat on the shore, mending their nets. In the distance, there was a horizon of white houses cornering the beach. Which, except for the two men, seemed deserted.

At that time, I had to go to the dentist every week, so that painting became my private obsession. I would spend all my time there watching it, since, on each visit, the painting told me a different part of the story.

First, it asked me to look at the faces of the fishermen, drenched in sweat and bearing an incredible resemblance to my grandfather Alfredo and his brother Pedro. Two sturdy men, their skin tanned by the sun and salt, with a half-smile that reflected the end of the day.

Then, I saw the details of the boat and the sand. The gold and the shadows. The net full of fish, the sponges thrown on the floor. The cracks. The buckets full of ice.

Subsequently, I noticed the colors of the painting, especially the blue of the shore and the white of the boat and the low houses. However, one of the houses was white, but had its entire facade covered with blue and yellow ceramic tiles. It was the one that stood out the most, even though it was hidden in a corner of the painting.

In that house you could see an open window and a man inside with no shirt and a huge knife in his hand. He could have been one of the murderers that appeared my comic books, but my grandpa had already shown me how to clean a fish, and I think that's what the man in the painting was doing.

The last week of my treatment, I already knew the painting off by heart. I could close my eyes and smell the saltpeter of the sea, the guts of the fish, the bread with oil put on the table and the toasted almonds in the kitchen.

Those two men had shared with me their secrets, telling me many stories of their adventures at sea.

I guess that painting marked my life and anchored me in a world of fish and salt that I refuse to leave in this hospital waiting room. Everything seems to sink, but the captain is always the last to leave the ship, or his boat.

«I think of myself more as a craftsman who modifies foods in terms of textures, combinations and proportions, because that is what cooking is all about».
Albert Adriá. TICKETS

THE CITY CIRCUS AND THE SUMMER OYSTERS

I thank whoever is up there for inventing the silent wagons. People still don't respect these anti-noise sanctuaries as they should, but at least you avoid being around those savages who love to listen to music without headsets or talk on the phone with the hands-free feature on.

Normally, I take the AVE Madrid-Barcelona to work, but today I woke up wanting to see the sea, and this train is like a magician who takes the rabbit out of his hat and leaves you open-mouthed. I know, I know, it is not a good time to set foot in Barcelona now that there are protests and more noise in the streets. When I walk around downtown, I have the feeling that I am a lion tamer in the midst of so much commotion, and I prefer to be a simple mime.

So here I am, heading to La Barceloneta, in the middle of a political crisis, in my polka-dot dress and my yellow flip-flops that almost killed me when I got off the train. Luckily, I'm kind of an acrobat ... Okay, who am I kidding? It was a miracle that I didn't fall. God didn't give me a good sense of balance, that's why I never ride a bike or juggle like that guy with dreadlocks at the exit of the station.

It's so hot that I can almost swallow the heat from the asphalt; that's why so many people come here from Madrid today, to escape from hell and run like bullets to take the shortest path to our destination of sand and salt.

I should have taken a cab, since the subway is full of idiots that make me wonder why there are no silent wagons here. Maybe people are not ready for that yet.

Just when my feet are about to touch the sand, I notice that my gut is roaring again. It's time for a beer and some oysters, because I feel glamorous today. The beach circus can wait, but not my stomach.

«But watching someone enjoy your food is the closest I've come outside of football to scoring a goal. It's the same feeling, the same thrill».
Bjorn Frantzén. FRANTZÉN

RIBS FOR THE HANGOVER

Ending up in this mile-long line while it snows incessantly is something I still regret. I vaguely remember the night before; I only recall many beers at Lan's house while we were playing an endless poker game. By the time the delivery guy arrived with the order, we were so drunk that we ended up inviting him to play with us, and I still don't remember how we convinced him.

We were five drunk guys losing imaginary money and debating about major life issues: Soccer and women. In one of those conversations meaningful only to the drunken, John began a monologue about the loss of values through technology and how we are dehumanizing ourselves. According to him, we would all end up being robots. All very profound, until Peter said that that was nonsense because robots would never know how to play soccer like Messi. After that, I don't remember how the conversation went to the Champions League final and how buying tickets online was a fool's errand. I think I mentioned that one could simply go to the stadium and buy them. The delivery guy, who was already one of the group, suggested that the next round should be played to determine who would buy the tickets in person, so as not to support capitalism through the Internet.

Sounds crazy, right? Well, last night I thought it was a great idea. Probably because of the alcohol, but also because of the frustration I feel in the virtual queues every time I want to buy tickets for an important concert. So, we bet that the winner of the next round got to choose who would go to the stadium to stand in line, for three days, until the ticket office opened to buy the tickets.

Long story short, someone won and chose me. So, here I am, in an endless queue with people crazier than me, lying on the floor with a chair and a blanket that I have borrowed. It's so cold that the thermos I've been given with coffee and something else now seems delicious, although not as delicious as the ribs and fries I'm craving right now. My favorite dish after a big hangover like this.

«I want to have things that only I will have».
Ángel León. A PONIENTE.

SEA MACKERELS

Murmurs among the public. Impatience is felt. The lights go out. A male voice introduces us. Nerves bursting. Silence. The curtain opens. The first chords are played. There is no presentation anymore, only the salty taste of our pasodoble.

The sea,
that cradles you in its arms,
sings to you,
sways you.
The sea,
so full of mysteries,
legends and stories.
The sea,
brave in the face of storms,
sea monsters and hurricanes,
lives in darkness and light;
it vibrates and feels, just like you,
proud of its blue blood.
The real boats,
only they are allowed to pass
because it has to feed them.
Years went by
and you are so far away.
Dead of jealousy,
and without your waves,
without your saltpeter,
without your lullabies,
without your sands.

You don't want treasures or to be a pirate anymore
because paradise is in its beaches
and in the rough waters that separate you.
The echoes of the south,
its winds, sirens, the lighthouse,
claim your youth.
Sardines, sea urchins and mackerel
fill your tongue with salt,
and algae cover your body, bathing you in the sea.

Be aware of the signal
and return to your sea waters that shed tears of salt.
Unhitch your boat and row,
do not fear the storm.
You both know that, in the end,
no one will stop you
from returning to the water.

«I don't want to build an empire and make money; for me, it's a much more personal matter».
Dani García. DANI GARCÍA GROUP (GRUPO DANI GARCÍA)

REFLECTIONS WITH A TASTE OF ESPETO

It is clear that very often we fail to value what we have on a daily basis, our treasures became invisible to our eyes.

I have always wanted to take on the world; I have had disproportionate ambitions and dreams and an exaggerated rebelliousness. Living in such a small town seemed to me like a divine punishment, and that's why I always found the perfect excuse to escape. College, a scholarship, a secret love, learning a new language, the economic crisis... anything was good enough to get me out of that piece of land that was suffocating my desire for freedom. And so I spent many years making a living out of anything, preferring to return home as a tourist.

What happened is that, when I stopped being a tourist in the host country, I became a tourist in my own land and began to see it with different and benevolent eyes. The endless breakfasts of my countrymen in the cafeteria became a slow life practice; the "levantera" no longer prevented me from going to the beach; being able to get to all places on foot was now an invaluable luxury; even the heat stopped seeming so horrible to me.

But what made me come back were the flavors of my land. Can you give up a flavor that you have barely tasted? It is easy for foreigners to forget about dishes that they taste only once a year, or that they eat in their own countries without knowing that they are being fooled. But what about the flavors that permeate our memories, those that are linked to a certain smell or sound? Those flavors simply can't be erased.

Don't be fooled. Globalization allows you to eat a pata negra ham at an affordable price on the other side of the world. But that ham, even if it's authentic, lacks the taste of the ruckus in the tavern; of the fight with your brother to see who will get the best piece; of the grandfather's lessons explaining how a good ham stands out from the rest. That mixture is what gives that ham its unique flavor.

You don't believe me? Give it a try with me. Take a plastic chair and sit by my side in this picnic area. Order a beer, or a tinto de verano, or a sangria. Whatever your body wants. Close your eyes when you take your first sip. Now drink. What does it taste like? My beer tastes like time standing still. Like that breath that refreshes your lungs and tells you that everything can wait a little longer. Like the lack of urgency. Like a freshness on the tongue. Like the foam blending with the sea foam in front of us. This, out of this place, doesn't happen. I took the liberty of ordering you some espetos, and maybe I should explain to you what it is first, or maybe you already know, but try it again with me. I'm sure you've eaten sardines before, but these ones have a unique taste. My espetos taste like saltpeter on the body. Like the sand on the feet. Like other people's conversations. Like a family sitting at a table. Like children playing around. Tell me now what your octopus tastes like, or tell me later about the taste of that rice pudding we are going to eat. If it doesn't revitalize you, you didn't have a good childhood or you weren't lucky enough to be from the South.

«At a restaurant, you're like a conductor in an orchestra. You're putting the stuff together in ways that nobody else can, or will».
«Minimizing leftovers is a matter of culinary creativity».
Dan Barber. BLUE HILL AT STONE BARNS

THE PARSNIP OF TRUTH

I knew the world was changing on February 2, 2020. I remember that date very well because the Super Bowl was played in Miami, and I was lucky enough to witness it live with my friend Susan. How I managed to get the tickets and see that final between Kansas and San Francisco is another story, but everything changed on that day.

That day I was so excited about the game that I didn't notice the subtle things that were happening around me. Like the compote that Susan's grandmother was preparing in the kitchen when I arrived at her house, or the debate that was being broadcast on TV. At that moment, I was only interested in the biggest show in the world, the one I had seen for years across the pond. All I could think of were the souvenirs I wanted to buy before entering the stadium, the cheerleader's dance, the celebrities I was going to see in disguise, the excitement before the national anthem, and that giant burger I was going to eat with nachos and Coke. Just thinking about it made my mouth water.

I wanted to be at the stadium five hours earlier, and Susan agreed because she didn't want to listen to me anymore. She would've liked us to enjoy the beach more, but I didn't want to miss anything. As soon as I arrived, I was surprised there weren't many people at the food stands, but I thought it was because it was too early and people usually have barbecues outside the stadium. However, there were only two or three groups at the barbecues, and the stands were half empty. Looking at the bags that people were carrying, I noticed that there were no obese people. I wasn't being judgmental, but statistically there are many fat people in the United States, and there, in the middle of the most incredible show in the world, there was no one with a few extra pounds. I was about to tell Susan about it, but when I went to the stalls to decide what greasy delicacy to buy, I was speechless. The burger stands were offering parsnip sandwiches, the pizza stands were serving vegetable pasta made on the spot, the nachos stands were selling baked potatoes and even the popcorn stands were offering seasonal fruit cones.

I was literally in shock! I couldn't breathe. They were stealing part of the essence of my day. And right then and there, I knew that if the cradle of junk food was changing like that, the whole world would be transformed sooner than expected. However, they could have implemented this healthy eating thing a little bit later and let me gobble up my junk food while watching the Super Bowl.

«We have been doing the same thing for generations, which is to put the environmental knowledge on the Paleolithic fire».

Aitor Arregi. ELKANO

MY GRANDFATHER'S TURBOT

I don't know how to say no to my nephew, that's why I am now on a bumper boat that is spinning on itself at a speed faster than my physical integrity can endure. I hope that today the Biodramina works better than when I was a child – I used to hide inside the boats of the fishermen of my neighborhood until they went out to fish. They turned a blind eye and I never learned. So, dizziness after dizziness, I convinced myself that the sea was not meant for me no matter how much I loved it, like most of the lovers I've had in my life.

I manage to save the guy in front of my four-year-old nephew, and the little one literally pushes me towards the food stands; there is no doubt that he is a member of the family: small, always with his soccer team's shirt and scarf, and putting food before toys or fairground attractions at such a young age.

He got his indecisiveness from me, that's why we've been walking around the stalls for half an hour. He's on my shoulders because he wants to see the dishes up close, even though he knows them by heart.

The spices of the Moorish skewers; the variety of the roast potatoes; the tenderness of the fried octopus; the salt of the toasted corn, and the grease of the burgers... But nothing is decided. Besides, I have to be careful with the stalls that have grills, since this child is hypnotized by the fire and the dance of the embers.

I'm getting hungrier and hungrier, and when my gut starts to growl, I feel like sending the kid to my sister. She's his mother, damn it!

As if reading my mind, dismantling my facade of exemplary uncle in the process, Xavi pulls my sleeve, tells me to get him down, points his tiny finger at me and whispers in my ear, "Let's go to Grandpa's house and play with fire."

Suddenly, I want to give him a big kiss, since that's his way of saying, "Let's go roast fish with grandpa." His innocence was a reminder of that child who always got seasick in boats, but loved the turbot that the sea gave him every day.

«Life is a journey. Some people snap photos along the way. Others write stories. Some sketch. I cook. That's the best way I know to experience what life has to offer at every turn».
Eric Ripert. LE BERNARDIN

THE LOBSTER FROM THE PAST

Like every morning for the past month, the sound of the bells indicates that the door has been opened, warning of danger and welcoming the spirits at the same time.

When the door opens, a very old lady appears and flashes a smile as enigmatic as Mona Lisa's, pulling a red curtain that hides a shop window full of esoteric objects as a hint to let potential customers know that they cannot be served at that time.

The man who has just entered follows the woman wearing the yellow turban with his head down, as if he were in a penitential procession. She, who is five feet tall, wears a silk gown with embroidered astrological symbols and radiates a serenity that enchants like a hypnotist. He, as tall as a skyscraper, wearing a pair of black jeans and a white cotton T-shirt, is so insecure that he looks like a teenager despite being in his fifties.

They both sit on very tall ebony chairs, facing each other and separated by a pink translucent plastic table. The room is small, the light is dim and they are surrounded by shelves that cover the walls from top to bottom, full of books and some objects similar to those in the window shop: Raw gems, porcelain figures, hourglasses and many candles of all colors and shapes.

Like it has happened for the past week, the old lady takes the man's left hand and runs her rough fingers along the lines of life, so smoothly that it tickles. However, today is Friday, and Friday is the day devoted to tarot cards. She takes off her turban and begins to shuffle the cards. He puts his right hand on the deck and closes his eyes, saying aloud questions for which he wants answers. She utters some words in a language he doesn't know and starts to place the cards face down, forming a kind of cross, on the table. Some major arcana come out and she starts to tell him a story.

She tells him about a sea that he crosses in an airplane. About a French farewell. About a restaurant surrounded by water. About a Playboy magazine. About Buddhist books. About an American love. About a terrible fall. About an almost mortal blow. About lobster dishes.

For a second, he remembers the taste of a lobster served on a very fancy plate. Then, he decides to believe in each of the fortuneteller's words, because, since he lost his memory, he needs to know everything about his past.

«The contemporary chef is much more than the sum of his recipes».
Massimo Bottura. FRANCISCAN OSTERIA (OSTERÍA FRANCISCANA)

CHARLIE'S TORTELLINI

The intermittent clicking of the tongue hitting the palate. Trembling hands. His childish smile. The curious look that checks the ingredients on the table. The choppy words. "*Nonna*, flour, salt." The clicking again. "Eggs, oil, water." His hands energetically kneading the ingredients as if his life depended on it. "Clock, rolling pin, table." He begins to dance rhythmically, as if it were a magical dance, while waiting for the necessary time to pass to stretch the dough. While the hands of his yellow clock move quickly, he begins to prepare the filling by reciting the ingredients three at a time. "Meat, ham, mortadella." More clicking. "Egg, salt, parmesan." Claps of excitement. Now the sauce. "Oil, onion, celery." He starts playing with his locks of hair. "Carrot, pepper, wine." He kisses his *nonna*. "Oregano, thyme, laurel." He hits the table several times. "Tomatoes, cheese, cheese." And he starts singing the song he learned at school about a mouse that eats cheese. He is tired. His *nonna* asks him to sit down and drink water. She knows the coming of her grandson's favorite moment, when he makes magic with his hands.

"Meatball, hazelnut, pellets." This is how he makes the filling that will go inside the pasta. "Square, center, triangle." And then he forms small triangles, sealing them with his fingers like the best of all artisans. His nimble fingers play with the tortellini until they have an imperfect shape, the most perfect for him. "Beautiful, perfect, delicious." He claps. "*Tortellini della nonna*."

His grandmother caresses his hair and gives him a kiss on the cheek, which is covered with flour. "Today, they're Charlie's tortellini." And then, laughing out loud, he hugs her so hard that they seem to melt like the cheese in his song.

SPICY

«Chefs are crazy, aren't they? All crazy people become chefs,
so I think I'm in the right profession».
Gaggan Anand. GAGGAN

THE CHILI AND HIM

It should be forbidden to do anything on Sunday mornings, especially during the winter. There's nothing like feeling the cold as you peek through the feather comforter, hiding again between the sheets to bask in their cozy warmth.

It's a shame to have such a large bed and be alone on days like today, when there are no clocks or alarms to dictate every minute of your life. It's great to be able to fool around while my senses awaken, but I have to admit, I miss him the most on Sunday mornings.

I can barely remember his features; his smell is long gone from this room. However, if I close my eyes, I can taste his body again.

I have never liked sweets or chocolate, so the first time he proposed me to use a chili pepper to explore and enjoy his body, I loved the idea. He would lie on his back and I would hold the chili pepper by the tail like a feather. Before I started playing, his body always tasted like bergamot oil, but after touching every corner with the chili, everything tasted like a mixture of chili and curry.

It was an exciting experience, and even more so as his body would bristle when I stopped in certain areas. The silence was sometimes broken by spontaneous gasps, and that ritual always ended with me biting the chili and giving him the hottest kiss of all.

Afterwards, we would listen to Kiss's "Lick it Up," which announced the beginning of an intense night of fireworks.

«A leader must be surrounded by valuable people who will not just say yes to everything he says, but who will question him and help him work on his weaknesses».
Enrique Olvera. PUJOL

THE IMPROVISED MICHELADA

Do you know that law, of which I don't remember the name, that says if something can go wrong, it will go wrong? I know that these thoughts go against all those philosophies that inundate our social networks, full of happiness and extra-positivism, but, come on, give me a break, today is definitely not my day.

It's no news that my morning at the office has been really shitty, that's no surprise. With a useless boss and some colleagues who fill my days with their complaints and lamentations, I just look forward to the day I can leave this place.

Nevertheless, despite this *wonderful* work environment, I had woken up today feeling positive and in a good mood, with a carefree attitude. I was looking forward to seeing Fran this afternoon, and I had high expectations. Big mistake, since expectations generally lead to disappointments. Fran is my most recent Badoo fling, and after a month of chatting on the app, then messages and phone calls that were a bit too intense, we finally agreed to go on our first date. Nothing formal, but since we're both foodies, Fran decided to book one of my favorite restaurants. I, in return, would wear the black lace thong that arouses him so much. It was a great plan, although I don't know if I'm more interested in seeing him or having that delicious mole for dinner. In both cases, my mouth was watering.

However, it seems that my positive attitude is not going to help me much today. My boss is behaving like a prick, more so than usual, and my colleagues are being as useless as ever; so, here I am, stuck in the office at seven in the evening when my date expects me on the other side of town in half an hour.

No one can say that I am not resolute. I intended to leave early today and walk to the restaurant to think about how my grand entrance would be, but considering this scenario, I have pretended to be sick. If I get an Uber quickly, I will be only five minutes late. What could possibly go wrong?

Well, to begin with, in the rush I forgot to put on my promised thong; I'm wearing a pair of granny panties, super comfortable, but the most anticlimactic thing in the world. When I got up from the chair, my pantyhose got stuck and now are useless. And, of course, I don't have an extra pair in my bag. But don't panic, Lola, you can take them off when you get to a bathroom and then act as if nothing had happened.

I'm telling myself all this while waiting for the Uber I've requested. It is horribly cold and it is starting to rain. Of course, I don't have an umbrella, so I hope that the car arrives soon. The app said it would take five minutes, but I ended up waiting for twenty minutes. I was about to cancel the service, but in that very moment the white Toyota that should have picked me up almost half an hour ago arrived.

No apology, no explanation. I get in and the driver starts the car, fueled by the adrenaline of the city. He can't imagine what I'll say in my review. Well, Lola, you need to breathe; you're only fifteen minutes late and Fran is already aware of the situation. I check the map every two minutes, but the driver and I must have different ones. Every time I look at it, the arrival time increases by five minutes. I was so worried about being late that I didn't realize that the man driving the Toyota doesn't know how to use Google Maps. Twenty minutes have passed, and now he confesses to me that he is more lost than the rice boat. Really?! I know that I'm not a human compass, but come on! At this point, I'm already an hour late, and I notice that Fran hasn't replied to my message yet.

While trying to tell the driver how to get to the restaurant, I decide that I'm going to call Fran. Five unsuccessful attempts and it keeps going to voicemail. Isn't that weird? He doesn't even care about my delay. When we are two blocks away, the car breaks down and stops in the middle of the road. Whoever's up there has to be doing this to me on purpose, seriously. I leave the driver with the breakdown and walk to the restaurant. At this point, no good can come out of what's left of the day.

Before entering the restaurant, I look through the huge window outside to see if I can spot Fran at a dinner table, but there's no sign of him. I don't know if he looks exactly like his pictures, but I think that if he were sitting there, I would recognize him. Nothing. I pluck up some courage and go in. A very young man tells me that there is no reservation in the name of Fran Montero. I ask him to check again. Nothing, but he says that tomorrow there is a reservation in that name. But what day is today? "It's the 4th, ma'am." Ma'am? I'm about to freak out. It's the 4th and not the 5th. Seriously, I don't even know the day I live anymore.

Of course, the restaurant is full and I can't order that mole, so the best I can do is go and get a cold michelada. That is, if I don't get lost again on the way. Universe, give me a break.

THE WINE OF DESIRE

She looks so sexy with that blindfold that I am not sure I will be able to restrain myself from jumping over the table that separates us right now. That loose hair, those unpainted lips, that black blindfold that deprives her of one of her senses to sharpen others, and the humidity of the cellar slowly seeping into our bones.

In front of her, two glasses of wine. And not an ordinary wine. I know that this time I am going to surprise her, even though she keeps complaining about such an ordinary plan, which she does every day: Wine tasting. She was expecting an evening of candles, vodka, mushrooms and caviar, but that can wait a couple of hours. She needs to start the evening with something different for her senses.

Pure silence, just our breaths and the wind banging on an old door that refuses to close. She takes the first glass from my hand, moves it gently, smells it and pours the contents into her mouth. She tastes it, passing the wine from one side of her mouth to the other with her tongue. Time seems to stop for a few seconds until she spits out the wine and then smiles. There is nothing that I wouldn't pay for that smile.

"I would swear they used carrots instead of grapes, but it tastes like that wine we tried once in Jerez, remember?"
"Yes, the palo cortado."
"What is this concoction, Vladimir?"
"Don't be impatient and try the second one."

86

Her curiosity has just been aroused, and that always wets her appetite, both physically and carnally. Now I am impatient too.

Again, she takes the second glass, which is identical to the previous one, and, after the ritual of movements and sniffing, she drinks a little of the wine, which provokes strange gestures on her face.

"This feels like tomato juice."
"Are you sure?"
"I said it feels like that, but it smells like roses."

After several minutes describing flavors and smells, she begs me to take off her blindfold. Impatience is eating her up. And when the cloth falls on the sandy ground, she notices the darkness of the cellar and the two bottles that have caught her attention so much.

"What is this?"
"A new experiment. You always complain about having to taste the same wines in your work. These are different. I have created them for you. They are yours."
"Yes, they are different. Are they made with vegetables?"
"Elementary, my dear Watson. Do you like them?"
"It's the most beautiful gift someone has ever given me. My own vegan wines."

Her smile was well worth the thousand failed experiments, and that small cellar witnessed how hunger and thirst made us devour each other ruthlessly and without waiting for dinner.

«I think Korean flavors are more of an acquired taste compared to other Asian cuisines».
Corey Lee. BENU

PADRÓN PEPPERS PT. 1

Everything was going as planned. My partner and I had studied our guest under a magnifying glass and knew what we had to do, what topics of discussion to bring up and where to go to make him feel like the king of the universe and achieve our goal.

We had picked him up in the morning at the airport, taking him to the hotel where he would stay, a 5-star superior hotel with only 10 rooms, something really exclusive. We gave him a couple of hours to rest and then took him to the area where we wanted to set up our business. He asked us a thousand questions about numbers, market studies and finances, but we dispelled all doubts with our answers and our excess of confidence. Neither the language nor the cultural differences were a problem in our meeting; John, my partner, was fluent in five languages and I had studied everything I could about our guest.

All that was left was to sign and shake hands to close the deal; so, when it was lunchtime, John and I looked at each other with relief and a sense of triumph. We were the perfect hosts in every respect. When we went to the restaurant we had booked, we wanted to impress our guest with a small private room and a surprise tasting menu. Since we knew he didn't like the waiters' explanations, we had agreed with them that they would simply bring the dishes and leave them on the table to be tasted. It was something that had never failed us and caused a very good impression on the guests.

While waiting for the dishes and drinks to arrive, we kept on talking about the remaining details and personal anecdotes. We were so confident that it took us a while to realize that our guest's face had changed color. Then, he began to look for something to put in his mouth. First a napkin, then a glass of water. He got up abruptly and went to the bathroom. Or so we thought. We were a bit bewildered by the hasty departure of our guest, but we never imagined that, instead of going to the bathroom, he would leave the restaurant and not come back. A waiter came twenty minutes later to inform us.

We were slow to react due to the absurdity of the moment, and when we decided to go and look for him, he had already left the hotel. At the reception, we were given a note that he had left for us. Still stunned by the situation, we didn't know how serious it was until we read the note: "Spicy is the devil."

At that moment, the look on my face was priceless. Although I had studied him thoroughly, I would never have imagined that a Mexican could not endure the spiciness of Padrón peppers. And that was how we lost the biggest deal of our lives.

«Simplicity is the hardest thing to achieve».
Thomas Keller. THE FRENCH LAUNDRY

PADRÓN PEPPERS PT. 2

When I used to tell people about my big plans, they all laughed and looked at me with pity. To them, I was just a crazy dishwasher. To me, they were just a bunch of unambitious buzzkillers. So, one day, I decided to stop talking and start working on my thing. I guess that fact increased the gossip about me and my mental well-being, but I'm so good at cleaning up the dirty dishes that the chef didn't care that I was no longer talking.

According to my mother, I am wasting my talent, but neither she nor anyone else can see the importance of my work. Cleanliness is essential. Or do filthy kitchens get Michelin stars? And I'm not just talking about the dishes, which I clean without the help of any machine, I'm also talking about the floors, utensils and everything else in the kitchen. This is not a job for the faint-hearted. You need a strong stomach to deal with all the things that need to be cleaned up every day, and you also require physical and mental strength to withstand such long shifts. I still remember all the times I threw up in my first week of work, and that coworker who ended up in the hospital for not taking the mandatory breaks. However, after passing the probationary period, everything got better.

The arrangement of the dishes; the rubbing of my hands; the running of the water; the foam of the soap; the sponginess of the sponge; the racket of the kitchen; the heat of the oven, and the shouts of the chef... All that is part of an exhaustive routine that frees my mind and has allowed me to work out a foolproof plan.

Today is an unusual day. The restaurant should be closed, but we have some special diners in the private rooms, and that means the chef is free to improvise the menu and cook whatever he wants. In fact, he and his team have been preparing all morning the dishes to be presented. Normally, the chef always listens to the suggestions of others, but this morning he arrived with a very clear idea of what he wanted to do. That scared me because the plan could be jeopardized. I started washing the dishes to think of an alternative that, after a moment, it came to me.

When the chef began to give the orders regarding the dishes for the evening, not many dared to propose ideas, considering the boss' decisive attitude. Then, I took advantage of the silence to utter something aloud while I continued with my cleaning task: "Today I have a craving for Padrón peppers." Everyone turned to look at me, some with their mouths open, not because of what I said, but because it was the first thing they had heard from my lips after three years of absolute silence. The shock lasted a few seconds, but it struck the chef enough to make him want to present a dish with those peppers, which happened to be available in the pantry.

Everyone has now returned to the usual rhythm of work, and I keep washing the dishes. The shift is about to start and everyone is at their posts for another perfect evening. Whenever I can, I discreetly look at the door, which opens and closes as the waiters come and go. From my position, I can see the room where three businessmen are dining. Two of them seem to be trying very hard to please the third one, and it looks like they are succeeding. The dish made with peppers is ready to be presented, and I look for an excuse to leave the kitchen and find a more suitable view. My whole plan depends on this moment.

The guest of honor finally eats one of the peppers. Now he hastily takes the glass of wine. Then the glass of water. The other two don't seem to notice anything, since they keep talking to each other. The man gets up from the table and I follow him. Everyone thinks he is going to the bathroom, but he rushes out of the restaurant and takes a cab. As if in an American movie, I also take a cab and ask the driver to follow that car. He looks at me weird for a second, but doesn't ask any questions and obeys. I will explain my absence later. Despite the adrenaline of the moment, I am not nervous, and even less so when I see the man heading for his hotel. I pay the cab driver and enter the hotel right behind the man, stumbling over him and almost making both of us fall to the ground. I apologize a thousand times and, without him noticing, I slip a business card into his jacket. Then, I pretend to have forgotten something in the cab and get out of the hotel. On the card, it was written: "Today the best dishwasher in the world, tomorrow the best chef."

I've been walking around the streets near the hotel for several hours now, and the more I wander, the more I see how flawed my plan is. Sometimes your mind plays tricks on you, and what seemed like a great idea, now seems absurd to me. My phone vibrates. I take the call. It's the man. After a while, I hang up. I regain my confidence. He wants to meet me. I smile. Well done. That's how you get the biggest deal of your life.

«We try to convey to the diners a sense of intimacy, care, and warmth. We welcome clients and say goodbye to friends».
Jorge Vallejo. QUINTONIL

THE CRUISE'S CACTUS SORBETS

I don't know who convinced me to get involved in all this. Well, I do know: My daughter Alma. If it had been anyone else, I would never have gotten on this ship. "It's going to be fun, Mom. It's like that TV show you saw with my grandmother. It's the kind of adventure you need to embark on." And now I'm on a Caribbean cruise, which may seem like a very exotic plan, but believe me, it's not that exotic.

Since I didn't want to travel alone, Alma thought it was a good idea to sign me up for a salsa cruise for singles. But, of course, she didn't consider my age, and here I am, being one of the grannies on the ship. Come on, it's a disaster. I don't have anything against the youth, but I'm not going to dance until the wee hours of the morning drinking only mojitos. And no, I'm not exaggerating. That's what I tried the first night, and the consequences were a terrible hangover and a messed-up knee.

So, having learned my lesson, my plan for the next ten days is to flee from the killer mosquitoes. From the nuisances whose only goal is to butter my bread. Even though I'm a lame old lady. And from the gunwale if I've drunk more than ten glasses of the magical elixir I discovered on this trip: Cactus and tequila sorbet.

I am drinking the fifth glass of the day and the captain informs us that we will stop in Cozumel to enjoy a day of diving. Diving! Ha! No way. And to top it all off, my skin is already red from so much sun. I'm running out of options and I'm only getting started. I shouldn't have listened to Alma!

A song by Celia Cruz is playing on the PA system and the boat is emptying. I get up from the hammock with my glass of cactus in one hand and my book in the other, protected by sunglasses as big as my face and a Pamela hat that is like carrying a neon sign that says: "Foreigner on vacation." Then, I head towards the side of the ship that frightens me much more than the ruthless pigeons in my neighborhood.

I see how all of them stand on the ground with their divine, tanned bodies and think about how nice it would be to be in my house, with my blanket and my cats. I let out a sigh. Anyway, I'm going to put my knee on ice for another while and drink another couple of sorbets. Afterwards, I'm going to visit that masseur who is such a Greek god and has hands that are pure magic (and not only his hands). This time I'll pluck up the courage to invite him to eat some beef tacos and drink some fresh micheladas.

Oh, Merche, the cactus is already going to your head! Either that, or it's the sunstroke. Whatever it is, I'd better keep away from the gunwale and see what the chef has prepared for today. If there are tacos al pastor, the matter is settled. The masseur and the rest of the world can wait a little longer.

«If you're a chef, you should know how to make bread or chocolate or salami. You don't have to be a master, but you should have an understanding».
Isaac Michale. THE CLOVE CLUB

PAKORA FOR DINNER

Imagine what it's like for someone with a bad sense of direction to come and live in a city like London. Add to that the fact that I've never been on a subway and I don't really know how to use Google Maps. Can you imagine? It's even worse. I'm one of those people who turns the map around to find the right direction; I get dizzy on buses; I don't know how to ride a bike, and my blood pressure drops when I'm in a crowd. Come on, I'm everything you could wish for.

Given this scenario, I have decided that the most favorable option is to get used to the London Underground as soon as possible, particularly avoiding the rush hour. And look, if you travel at odd hours like eleven in the morning or three in the afternoon, the ride can be quite peculiar.

If I'm not in a hurry, like now, I always wait for an empty subway car, to avoid possible blackouts and to be able to sit down. Even if I have a choice, I'll scan for the right person to sit next to, judging them as travelling companions. At night, I do this as a precaution, and during the day, to avoid boredom.

One of the things I like most about London is its cultural diversity: people from all over the world speak a plethora of languages there, wearing many different faces. As I'm a very curious person, or a gossiper as they would say in my town, I like to sit next to people that I see occupied with something, like this Indian woman who is using her phone as if her life depends on it.

Truth is, I can't help it, nor do I want to. Besides, the phone is so big and I'm so close that I can see everything she's doing perfectly. She's group-texting on WhatsApp, reading the *Hello!* cover, buying clothes on the Harrods website and creating a shopping list - what a way to make the most of your time!

My culinary vocabulary in English is a bit deficient, so I take my time reading the ingredients she writes in the app: chickpea flour, coriander, turmeric, garam masala, garlic, onion, eggplant, cauliflower, broccoli ... As I am just that bored, I start writing the ingredients on my phone, immediately growing hungry and thinking about tonight's dinner. I never know what to prepare for dinner, and here they don't have Mercadona. I copy and paste the ingredients in Google and I get the recipe to prepare pakora. I have no idea what it is. According to the photos, it's a dish that consists of fried vegetables, and it looks very good.

I realize that I've arrived at my stop. I try to make eye contact with the woman, but she's absorbed in her phone. It's a shame, I wanted to at least smile at her to thank her for solving my dinner problem tonight.

«Never underestimate the ability of the eyes to deceive the mind. What you see is not always what you get».
Massimiliano Alajmo. LE CALANDRE

A TORTUROUS DESSERT

There are many forms of torture, and some of them can produce such strange pleasures that I always wonder how our brain works, since it gives us such opposite sensations with the same action.

Everyone who knows me knows that I am a gourmand. A disaster in the kitchen, but with such a developed palate that no one was surprised when I decided to become a food critic. I soon made a name for myself in this world of egos and vanities, which has the taste of cigar smoke, because of my knife-sharp tongue and my stunning heels. I ended up traveling all over the world and visiting the best restaurants, or those that the stars and trophies qualified as such.

After a few years, the dishes became increasingly boring, and my interest shifted to small restaurants, steakhouses and even street food stalls that no one had ever heard of. They were my little discoveries, giving me a satisfaction that dethroning the best of the best had lost.
It was really difficult to surprise me, in life and in the kitchen, until I met Rafa. He was a cook with a hidden trattoria in a lost village, to which I arrived by chance one day when a tire on my car was flat. It was late and there was only one free table, with diners tasting slowly their tiramisu. I asked if the kitchen was still open and they sat me at a table, next to a window, that allowed me view of it every time the door opened.. I was so hungry that I agreed to have whatever the chef wanted. Anything that didn't

require too much time to prepare. When I finished the five courses and awaited dessert, I noticed I was the only one in the trattoria. Well, me and whoever was in the kitchen. Suddenly, I couldn't see any of the waiters who had been serving me like a queen.

Maybe I had drank too much wine, since my eyes began to blur and I felt my body getting heavier and heavier. I even thought I had nodded off, but when I tried to open my eyes, I could only see black and feel velvet on my eyelids. My hands were tied behind my back, and the lack of sight automatically caused the rest of my senses to heighten. I could hear a very soft melody and footsteps. I was supposed to be scared, but I was just curious and missing my dessert. I couldn't see, but the table smelled of freshly baked bread, freshly picked tomatoes, olive oil, and appetizers made with parmesan. I felt I could eat again, and my mouth was savoring the pasta I had swallowed a while ago. I felt a hand bringing different smells to my face: oregano, garlic, basil ... and a hot liquid spilling down my neck. They were cooking over my body! Those smells and the touch of the food on my skin made me hungry, and only when I started to let go of the ropes did someone come up to me and put their tongue in my mouth, depositing something that tasted like cookies, coffee and mascarpone. It was torturing my palate. Rafa approached (I didn't know who he was then) and whispered something in my ear in Italian. He was going to be my dessert and my torture. A delicious torture.

«It is about me. Honestly, when people ask me who my cooking hero is, I say no one. I am my own cooking hero».
Ana Ros. HISA FRANKO

A RAVIOLI-SHAPED DECISION

Just then, Julia realizes that being a good diplomat has nothing to do with studies and languages. She should tell that to her mother, but she hasn't spoken to her for months, and those thoughts never appear in the middle of an argument. Those thoughts appear an hour later when you are home alone.

She is standing in the middle of a room full of unfinished tables and people running around nervously. She exhales briefly, lifting her blonde bangs. Then, she freezes the image around her, stopping time to pay attention to all the details. Naked tables, tablecloths piled up and waiting to be spread out; cutlery and crockery waiting to be cleaned; two children crawling on the floor; a husband with whom she has an ongoing argument; a phone ringing with no one to answer it; notebooks full of numbers and problems waiting to be solved; half-finished recipes and a half-open kitchen full of tension and speculation.

She blinks and everything goes back to normal. Julia decides to sit down and start making decisions. It is apparent that her method doesn't work; she lives in complete chaos because she always tries to mediate and carry out the work of a team alone. She is going off the rails, but she is more than willing to get back on track.

She enters the kitchen and prepares ravioli filled with trout and chili broth, watched by her entire team. Nobody says a word. They do so out of fear; she remains silent because she is focused on her thoughts. That dish is part of her personality, of her history, and she is telling it like it really is.

She knows what she has to do, and she has been putting it off for months. She feels betrayed by a person she loved and trusted, who has deceived her for too long. It doesn't matter what anyone else says, not even her husband. She is not going to forgive that infidelity or let them steal what is hers. Her kitchen.

«It's always good to reanalyze everything».
Luke Dale - Roberts. THE TEST KITCHEN

THE ONION DANCE

Once, at an awards gala, I was asked for the umpteenth time where my passion for dance came from. I always answered the same thing: "Of course, not from my family." My father was a cook, my mother a lawyer, and my grandparents had been farmers, teachers and bankers. There was absolutely nothing in the family background. I guess it was all a matter of coincidence led me to sign up for ballet classes as an extracurricular activity. Nothing worthy of a Hollywood biography. I don't know why, but despite all the success I had achieved, it secretly still bothered me that I didn't have a legacy of dancers behind my back. At home, we didn't listen to music regularly and only danced at weddings and New Year's Eve. Everything was very vulgar.

I had been living abroad for many years, always touring and performing all over the world, but a knee injury forced me off the stage for a few months and my mother had insisted that I should return home for a while. Maybe dancing wasn't their thing, but the power of persuasion was a family legacy, so I had no choice but to return as the prodigal daughter for a few weeks.

And here I am. After a fourteen-hour flight, I get into a cab to go to my parents' house, feeling unhinged and having dark circles under my eyes. Without any reason, I decide to surprise my father, so, instead of going home, I go straight to the restaurant. It's early, but I'm sure he must be there preparing the lunch service with his team.

As if I am a mischievous little girl again, I sneak in through the back door that is always open and hide behind a hole that allows me to watch the scene that is unfolding.

101

The music in the background sounds lively, with percussion and African rhythms. Even though the others don't seem to notice it, I do. I see how all the people working in that kitchen move in coordination under the influence of the tune. Some bend down looking for utensils while others dodge them by doing a pirouette to save the freshly made salsa. Someone sharpens the knives while moving his feet in an attempt to dance salsa and another man stretches his arms to reach a dish that is too high. I see a plié when someone opens the oven and feet in fourth and fifth position performed by those who are cutting the vegetables. And I see my father in the background, chopping onions with his very sharp knife while moving his hips to the beat of the drums.

I come out of my hiding place and go to where my father is, giving him a big hug. The next time someone asks me where my passion for dancing comes from, I will say, "From my father's kitchen."

BITTER

«You need to look for what is not obvious».
Rashus Kofoed. GERANIUM

THE CANDY OF DEFEAT

It is said that candies are always sweet, but I still remember vividly the most bitter candy I've ever eaten in my life.

I was eight years old, and it was a family tradition that my grandfather, my father and I went to the soccer stadium on Sundays to watch the game. It was the best time of the week, and we prepared ourselves thoroughly. My father and I would go to my grandparents' house for breakfast, where my grandmother waited for us with a table full of different kinds of bread and freshly made cupcakes. Scents of a wood-fired oven filled the house. When we entered, the heat of the flames would embrace us almost as strongly as she did.

When we sat at the table, she would leave the three of us alone to talk about our things. Well, it was more like my father and grandfather explaining how the coach should lead his team while I listened to them and devoured as much candy as I could. That morning was really important because the Super League final was between our team and Silkeborg. You could feel the tension in the air and in the little details, like when my father raised his voice more than usual to discuss with my grandfather which players should be on the field that day.

When the discussion lasted for too long, my grandmother would always appear as a referee to put things in order. He'd prepare the bag with candies and food that we always took to the stadium. She never forgot to put in my favorite one: a chocolate turtle filled with cream, caramel and rum.

That afternoon we entered the stadium earlier than usual to avoid the long queues and because we didn't want my father to get nervous. It was an important day, and we all knew it. It wasn't about winning; for my grandfather it was a matter of pride, to reward the fighting and competitive spirit of our team.

It was a tense game, one of those that take your breath away. Many fouls and many shouts to end up in what I feared most: The penalty round. I had almost finished the whole bag of candies, leaving my favorite chocolate for the end, as always. I hesitated between eating it and leaving it for the return home, but my anxiety pushed me to open it and take the first bite.

I remember everything in slow motion. The sound of the paper tearing between my fingers; my grandfather sitting facing the ground; my father standing with his hands on his head; the stadium in complete silence; the last penalty that would decide the champion; the player kicking the ball; the piece of chocolate in my mouth; the ball approaching the post; my tongue savoring the cream; the ball touching the post; my grandfather covering his face and biting his lip; my father jumping; the ball out of the goal, and my favorite candy tasting as bitter as the defeat we had just witnessed.

«The vital ingredient of Den is people. Those people include our team, our customers, our suppliers and our producers».
Zaiyu Hasegawa. DEN

THE TEA CEREMONY

Being the eldest of four children means becoming a father to your siblings prematurely. I have always been a very responsible kid, and every time my mother smiles at me for looking after them, my heart beats faster. Sometimes I don't have enough patience to convince them to do their homework or eat all their food, and today is one of those days. I tell Mizuki to stay with Ryu and Kai and, in exchange, I'll give her some candies I have hidden in the kitchen. Then, I leave the house.

It's the first time I've done something like this, and I hope Mizuki can keep a secret, otherwise I'll get in trouble. I start walking without knowing where to go, and in the end, in no time, I end up at the *ochaya* where Mom works. I have always wanted to know what she really does and, even though my grandmother always tells me stories about Mom's work, maybe today I can see it with my own eyes.

I know that there is a window in the back, where, if I manage to climb the mountain of wood scraps, I can see what happens inside the *ochaya*. It's not easy to hide on top of that wood without losing your balance, but thank goodness I'm small and can hold on to the frame of the balcony. Yes, there's mommy! She looks like someone else with that elegant suit and her face painted white.

I can also see a *tatami* room and a paper sliding door. There are several barefoot men who have entered the room through a corridor surrounded by a small garden. They are all wearing silk kimonos in plain colors and *tabis*.

I have to be more careful now, since a boy a little older than me has pulled down the reed curtains that cover the windows on the outside. I look for another window and I see Mom again. It must be the preparation room, because she's organizing the necessary things for the ceremony.

I am mesmerized by her movements. Her delicate hands move gracefully as she cleans the tea pot and ladle with a *fukusa*, then rinsing the stirrer in the tea pot after pouring hot water. Next, she pours that water into another pot and cleans the first one with the *chakin*.

Each step of the ceremony is like the magic tricks my grandfather does at home. Each movement is unique, and time seems to stand still. Mom goes back to the previous room and I look for another window to see her. After lifting the ladle and the tea pot, she puts the *matcha* in the pot. Then, she fills the ladle with hot water, which she takes from the pot placed on the fire, pours said water into a cup and returns the rest to the pot. Next, she shakes the mixture with the bamboo stirrer until the *koicha* appears. It's like my grandmother always says, but there's something special about the atmosphere that I can't grasp the words for.

Mom puts the pot in the right place, near the brazier, and the main guest, a very elegant man, moves using only his knees to take the cup. This guest bows to the others and places the cup in the palm of his left hand, holding it on one side with his right hand. He takes a sip, says that it tastes very good and takes two more sips. Then, he wipes the part of the cup that he has touched with his lips with the *kaishi* and passes it to the next guest, who does the same. The cup is passed around to all the guests so they can drink some of the tea. When the last guest finishes, he gives the cup back to the main guest, who hands it to Mom to take everything out of the room. When she bows silently, everyone knows that the ceremony is over, but I am still hypnotized and hidden behind the window.

I assume that many hours have passed. My legs hurt from being hidden for so long, but it was worth it. Now I am the only one of my brothers that has seen Mom at work and knows the secret of that ritual they call *the tea ceremony*.

«There is a new generation that is trying to find a meaning to their life, to the way they live, to what community they belong and are proud of. Something that will help us eat even better».
Heinz Reitbauer. STEIRERECK

THE BITTER ORANGE

My wife doesn't think I can be left alone with the baby, and I think that's an exaggeration. Okay, it's true that she has this maternal instinct that gives her the right answer for every situation that arises with Mateo, whereas I always end up messing things up. But I'm the official family disaster, that's what I'm supposed to do. Besides, I want to be a fun dad, one of those folks who goes on Facebook and has fun with their kids.

So, after a lot of whining and pleading, Elena has agreed to go to the gym for a couple of hours and leave me in charge of house and baby. I'm the king of the castle, but with an endless list of rules, instructions and assumptions. An earthquake may strike and I'm sure Elena has something written down on that list about what to do.

Everything is under control. Baby food already prepared, a pile of diapers at hand, clean clothes and suitable toys. Supposedly, Mateo will be sleeping the two hours that his mother is out. However, the baby detects that his momma is not home with some kind of magical baby radar and decides that he wants to party or eat. Well, no, he is actually crying because he needs a new diaper. So, once I put on my nose clip and surgical gloves, I go on a "butt wiping" mission.

After two attempts, Mateo has a new diaper on, and now I can tell that he's hungry. I sit him down in his highchair and start preparing the baby food. Well, I'm just going to warm it up, but now I have forgotten the ideal temperature, so I go and get the list of instructions that Elena has left for me in her infinite wisdom. When I'm about to pick it up, I see an orange from the garden in the fruit bowl; they are a somewhat rare species, like us, and bitter. Then, I conceive a great idea.

In the end, the baby food has dried up, but it seems that Mateo is not really hungry; he just wants to play with his daddy. I take advantage of the fact that he's sitting in the highchair and give him half of the orange. At first, he thinks it's one of his toys, due to that bright color, and then he discovers with his fingers that there is a softer part and that, if he squeezes it, some liquid comes out. He is happy with his new discovery. When I see that he is about to investigate the orange with his teeth, I take out my phone and start recording. His face changes drastically when he tries to bite the orange and discovers bitterness for the first time. It is priceless. I have to upload this to YouTube. And yes, I know, Elena is going to kill me when she finds out.

«A cook has to have the curiosity of a collector».
Yannick Allenó. ALLENÓ PARIS AU PAVILLON LEDOYEN

THE SECRET IN THE BEARNAISE SAUCE

When the police arrived at the crime scene, it seemed pulled from a Tarantino film or Salvador Dali's imagination. It was an open space, with no partitions. Rooms painted in bubblegum pink. In the middle, there was a perfectly secluded and unpolluted kitchen island that contrasted with the chaos that prevailed in the rest of the place.

There was no relevant furniture, only a shelf that covered the entire wall from top to bottom, three huge sofas, a projector and a record player on a marble table, all in indigo blue. On the floor there were five people dressed delicately in 16th century costumes. They appeared as though they were asleep, if not for the pools of blood that accompanied each of the lifeless bodies. The record player was playing Bizet's "Carmen", and on one of the walls the film *Kill Bill* was being projected without sound. Next to the bodies, there were empty champagne glasses and half-eaten colored pasta.

In the middle of the cleanest kitchen in the world, a red-haired man dressed in a blood-stained chef's uniform held a Japanese knife in his left hand. With his right hand, he obsessively beat a bowl while endlessly repeating the instructions of what seemed to be a cooking recipe:

"... ¼ cup of white wine vinegar, ½ cup of white wine, 2 chopped shallots, 1 fresh tarragon leaf, 4 egg yolks, ¾ cup of melted and warm butter, 1 tablespoon of fresh and chopped tarragon. Salt and pepper. My father used to tell me the recipe that my great-

111

grandfather Collinet had invented every night, but don't ask me about the secret ingredient in the sauce. Because if you do, I will have to kill you all."

«Just because something's traditional doesn't mean it can't be improved. Only knowledge allows you to make that tradition evolve».
Rodolfo Guzmán. BORAGÓ

THE PLUM PIE

Everyone in town viewed Peter's journey as a madness. He left everything: his job, home and family to cycle around Patagonia with no return date. He'd always had an adventurous but repressed soul, and for him, leaving his boring job at the post office, his tiny apartment and his distant relatives was the best decision he had ever made. One of those decisions that are made on impulse and without looking back in order not to let doubt creep in.

Pedro's decision was made on a Sunday morning when he was cleaning up at his recently deceased grandmother's house. She was the only family he had left, and now that she was gone, it was his turn to put everything in order. A life of memories scattered in hidden boxes and old photographs.

Feeling very unenthusiastic, Pedro put a The Ramones record in his CD player and started throwing away everything that didn't make sense to keep. He wasn't very sentimental, or so he thought. By the time he went into the kitchen, the house was already naked and cold, devoid of almost everything. He had left the kitchen for last, since he knew that she kept her most precious things there: Her recipe books. Shabby notebooks that she had written throughout her life, still smelling of her and the plums she loved so much.

Suddenly, he was no longer in a hurry to finish. He had found an unfamiliar recipe book hidden in a drawer full of junk. It was yellow, almost the same as its pages, and although it looked very old, it was well preserved. There, he found the recipe for one of his favorite desserts, and as though his grandmother were still there, he realized that all the ingredients he needed were in that kitchen: Plums, milk, and even myrtle. Without thinking twice, he finished reading the recipe and started cooking. It was his favorite dessert because his grandmother had created it for him when she discovered that he was the only child who did not like chocolate.

While he was cooking, he found a loose note in the middle of some pages. He could tell it was his grandmother's shaky, almost unrecognizable handwriting. Even though he could barely read a few sentences, the final words were the ones that stuck in his head: "To know where you are going, you must know where you come from and who you are."

When the dessert was finished, he put the notebook in his backpack and decided to go away in search of his purpose. That was the sign he had been waiting for, which his grandmother sent him in the form of a pie.

«Those who say that haute cuisine is expensive should check how much the phone they have in their hands costs».
Josean Alija. NERUA

NIGHTMARE AT BREAKFAST

I eventually gave in, and here I am sitting in the waiting room of the psychiatrist Julen recommended. Only he knows that I'm here, and not by choice, really. He insisted so much when we were at the *txoko* that I ended up telling him I'd come. I don't know if it was simply to keep his mouth shut or because I overdid it with the *txakoli*.

I don't like waiting rooms. Does anyone like them? In this one, I feel like I'm in a slaughterhouse. I feel like I'm waiting for someone to invite me in so that I can undress in front of a stranger who will end up laughing at my confidences as soon as I walk out the door.

I'm about to leave when a woman says good morning to me and asks me to come in. Her face is stern, probably in her forties, with a perfectly straight mane. She is wearing a navy-blue jacket and skirt. I don't know why, but she scares me.

I sit on a chair in front of her, still staring at her, and the most uncomfortable minutes of my life begin. For some strange reason, she doesn't say anything and we just look at each other. I don't know what to say, so I start to move around in my chair, which seems smaller than usual.

"How does this work? Aren't you supposed to ask me questions?"
"You are here to tell me what you want, and I am here to listen."
"So, it's like paying my neighbor, who already hears my conversations through the walls."

"If you want to see it that way..."

"I don't want to see it in any way, I want you to solve the problem. If you can give me a magic pill, that will suffice."

"That's not how it works"

"That's the first thing I asked you. How does this work?"

"Tell me why you came here."

"I came here because I overdid it with the *txakoli*, and because Julen is such a pain."

This is going to take longer than expected, so I let out a sigh and start telling her what's been happening to me every night for the past few months. It's always the same thing. It's harder than usual for me to fall asleep, and when I do, my mind believes everything I dream about. One day I dreamt about being a writer, and when I woke up, my hands were paralyzed. Another day, I was a soccer player, and when I opened my eyes, I couldn't move my legs. Same thing every night: A blind painter, a deaf musician, a philosopher with no memory ... And each time my mind believed it to be true for longer, making it really difficult to recognize they were just nightmares.

The truth is, what brought me here today was not Julen or the *txakoli*, it was what has been happening to me for the last five days. One morning, the alarm clock rang and I went to prepare my fruit, yogurt and espresso breakfast. I didn't remember being anyone other than myself, so I thought the nightmare stage was over. The noise of the coffee maker warned me that the espresso was ready. I quickly realized that the bowl with fruit and yogurt didn't taste of anything. I was more nervous with each bite. I opened the fridge and started to taste everything inside. Milk, anchovies, ham ... Nothing. I had lost my palate.

Since then, the days keep passing by and I don't know how to make my mind understand that I can't be a chef who doesn't recognize flavors.

«I like to think that the C.V. is irrelevant. Passion is the most important trait to have in a kitchen».
Paul Pairet. ULTRAVIOLET BY PAUL PAIRET

DARK CHOCOLATE

Elvira had been in charge of preparing everything, taking care of every detail, including leaving the dog with the neighbor from the fifth floor. They'd eaten a delicious menu, with the right number of calories, under the light of electric candles. Accompanied by the mythical songs of Frank Sinatra. The house smelled of jasmine, and the open windows let a breeze flow in that hot summer night.

They finished the wine and it began to have an effect on their words, making them more daring and melting the shyness of the lovers. They were so sensitive to touch that Elvira slowed down the caresses, slightly rubbing her fingers and saying phrases that made her partner drool. The last drops of wine vanished between their tongues, tired of speaking and impatient for the final dish.

Elvira got up first to bring the chocolate fountain. They noticed the unexpected power cut thanks to the alternator, but it didn't matter to them because they knew the path off by heart, the path to the house and the path to their lips. Right there, on the table, the first kisses and whispers were heard. And the first surprises also arrived. While embracing each other, they noticed that neither of them had their clothes on, and they laughed because they had had the same idea. Who needs to see a lace lingerie, when you can touch the softness of a skin that smells like orange and cinnamon? Who feels the skin bristle and decides to stop to go to bed? They certainly didn't. The table became their game board, and the melted chocolate became the paint that would travel across the canvas of their bodies.

Thus, the night was tinted with different shades of black: The black of the coffee waiting to be drunk; the black of the elegance of that night; the black of the tablecloth turned into a sheet; the black of the everlasting darkness of their eyes, and the black of the melted chocolate waiting to be devoured by their tongues.

«My cooking is the result of my experiences in a country afflicted by conflict, of my passage through the different communities that feed my soul».
Leonor Espinosa. LEO

THE ANTS OF FREEDOM

The same hour. The same eye booger in my eyelashes. The same hopeless yawn. The same shower. The same unwillingness. The same sugar-free coffee. The same bag. The same bus. The same bus stops. The same window displays. The same concrete that colors the streets. The same route. The same elevator. The same faces. The same uncomfortable chair. The same blinding screen. The same emails. The same meetings. The same calls. The same sheep from the flock.

This was supposed to be different. I work with creators who should have wild ideas and daily dramas instead of bland, copycat occurrences. Advertising is a lie; it disguises itself as a sweet candy until you realize it's one of those that taste like medicine.

Sometimes I need to have a drink to survive this dullness. Other times, I paint naked virgins screwing fluorescent archangels while listening to Quinta Guajira. And on other occasions, I look for some kind of conflict that allows me to camouflage myself in this country of violence and cumbia.

Today is one of those days when I need to sniff a line in the bathroom to be able to function. You may think that this is not very professional of me, but in this agency, it is like drinking a glass of water. Besides, it allows me to get away from the noise of the computer keys, the phone that never stops ringing and the empty conversations. It allows me to focus on other things that are more important, like the row of ants that run around my desk.

They are so perfect, so submissive, so orderly, on a very important mission. They travel slowly through my body, producing a sensation that paralyzes me for a moment until they melt into my skin to feed my soul. They tickle me. They are steady in their purpose, crunchy, with a flavor of peanuts that mixes with my blood to erupt and pull me out of here.

If I had wings, I would fly. However, I slowly pick up my stuff and watch the same emails, the same blinding screen, the same uncomfortable chair, the same faces and the same elevator for the last time.

«A chef is only a part of who I am, he said. It's not all that I am. I am me, he concluded. Just like everyone is».
Heston Blumenthal. THE FAT DUCK

ICE CREAM ON THE BEACH

Today is my birthday, although there are no candles to blow out. I stopped making wishes a long time ago. Besides, I can always go back to the time I was afraid of seagulls, and swimming at the beach was the best remedy to avoid colds during the winter.

My wet swimsuit is glued to my body. There is sand on my feet. I hear other people's conversations coming from the nearby towels, the roar of the waves, the screams of mothers with no patience, the can of soda opening. I smell the cold potato omelet sandwich, the peaches we're going to have for dessert, the afternoon pipes. And my tongue is bathing in melted ice cream, which drips down my cheeks and my sticky hands.

I take my headphones off and all the sounds of the sea are silenced, no more seagulls, no more waves. I open my eyes and the shore full of shells disappears. There are still no candles to blow out. I get up and go back to my cell before the robots force me to eat that garbage, empty of memories.

«I always notice the smell of a restaurant and the smiles of the people who are eating there».
José Andrés. JALEO

THE BITTER TASTE OF MEMORIES

I don't remember my decision to go away forever as something very thoughtful. And I'm very glad I didn't think it through, because the longer you think about things, the more space you leave for fears and doubts to change your mind.

In my case, the crisis that was shaking the country was not the reason for me to go and live abroad. It was simply the lack of motivation in a business that always threatened to close down and that restless desire to find my place in the world. I had always known that that particular piece of land could not be the only thing awaiting me in life.

I had less than three months to: Say that I was leaving, do the numbers, do a little research regarding the arrival, figure out how to prepare a suitcase for the occasion and take the plunge. Believe me, the less you think about it, the better.

I suppose that the first stages of this trip began during those months. The first time I was leaving without knowing when I would return; the first time I was saying goodbye to people without knowing how long it would take to see them again; the first time I was making arrangements in another language... I was experiencing an adrenaline rush that only allowed me to see all the good things that could happen. Excess of optimism and lack of experience, those things would change in less than twelve months.

But let's go back to my departure date. I always skip to the end when I tell this story, although, come to think of it, this one in particular doesn't have one yet.

I didn't weigh up the pros and cons very well because I thought that there weren't many cons, and that all the pros were enough to make me leave a place that no longer had much to offer. I have to admit it, I came back to stay one summer that ended up lasting four years, but it was time to go.

I prepared myself to survive a few months, carefully studying my first steps. However, reading forums and blogs on the internet is one thing, but the reality you encounter when you set foot on solid ground is a whole different matter. And it is necessary to live it, because many details can get lost.

I remember the nervousness of the previous night, the time I closed that heavy suitcase, the goodbyes of the previous days and the feeling that a three-hour flight wasn't the end of the world. I shouldn't feel sad, like the people I was leaving behind.

Then, to lift my spirit and give me strength, I thought about how boring the place I was leaving behind was and the routines that were slowly disappearing; I decided to focus on the immense future that was unfolding before me. All those thoughts kept me busy for a while, but sooner or later the Earth shakes your foundations, and those memories became a paradise that I missed and hated at the same time.

I remember the nervousness I felt when I arrived, the journey to that house where I would sleep the first nights, the coldness of March, the color of the clouds, the weight of the suitcase, the tiredness and the feeling of uncertainty that you get when you don't know what will happen tomorrow. That same feeling that frees and scares you at the same time.

The first failures proved to me that starting a new life in another country is never easy, no matter how well prepared you may be. There will be a lot of things you don't know about that new culture, and you'll discover them for yourself as the months go by. This is told to you by a woman that can't be labeled as the typical Andalusian who is in love with her land. And even so, I found great differences.

When you realize that you are no longer a tourist and try to be one of them, the frustration begins. I think that's a big mistake; you don't have to be one of them, you just have to adapt to their rules and coexist. Your essence is something unique and no one should ever make you feel less for being different. Always be proud of your roots, your accent, your humor, your traditions. Be humble enough to absorb things like a sponge and enrich yourself, but never allow them to make you believe that they are better than you, because I promise you, they are not.

Sometimes you'll be your own worst enemy, thinking you are not cut out for this. You'll feel that everyone is giving you a hard time, that you keep walking backwards without any hope of reaching your goal. During those moments, breathe deeply and remember that you don't have to rush things, you need to be consistent and never give up. You need to remember that you are braver than many, that first times are always scary, but they're also exciting. You need to remember that now you have more possibilities before you than you had a few months ago. You draw the line, not others. After that, it's a matter of a lot of effort and a little bit of luck (because I still believe that luck exists and comes to those who seek it).

And just as you don't let anyone mess with your family, even if what they're saying is true, you become the best defender of your land, and the bitter memories disappear. You praise that plaza, which is small but full of life in the mornings. You remember all the places that, even though they are closed, were an essential part of your life, such as the Magallanes cinema, the Isa ice cream parlor or the McDonald's on Ancha street. The eternally polluted beach becomes a box of childhood and teenage memories, like the mornings you spent there with your grandmother or your first kisses. And the two main streets become the arteries that give life to the endless chats between friends, to the tapas that are eaten in bars as an excuse for hugs and toasts, and to Ani's squid as the dish that takes you home, even if it's only for a few days.

SAVORY or UMAMI

«My only ambition is to love what I do more and more every day. My garden saved my life».
Alain Passard. ARPÈGE

THE EGGPLANT PAINTING

There are painters who need external inspiration to give life to their canvases, but I don't need to leave these four walls for the muses to come and visit me. Even today, the image that of the living room when I woke this morning is the perfect print to recreate with my watercolors

All the windows in the main room are open, letting the curtains dance with the wind, intertwining the sounds of the outside with those of the kitchen and the music that John is playing using his saxophone.

In the distance, you can see the Eiffel Tower. And if you look closely from the balcony, the small home garden gives contrast to the crazy 1920s vibes of the city.

The living room is an open space without divisions of any kind, which welcomes anyone who needs a break from the hectic pace of everyday life.

John also paints my canvas with his improvised music, using colorful notes that give life to the scene I'm creating.

Laura is lying on a high table, receiving a massage. She seems to be asleep, but I know her mind is somewhere far away, dreaming of green palms and crystal-clear waters or maybe something else. My mind, on the other hand, has been focused on the vigorous hands of her masseur, on his nimble fingers pressing her whitish skin, weaving in a slippery way through the nooks and crannies of her back. Hands that revive muscles, heal wounds and tell stories. Magic hands.

This life of notes, dances and rhythms highlights the colors of the grand piano keys, the cushions that decorate the giant sofa and the carpet that invites us to walk barefoot.

I have the perfect romantic setting, but it is the aroma coming from the kitchen that unleashes my inspiration, giving me the colors I was looking for.

Today, Grandma is playing with eggplants and tomatoes, dyeing the final scene with red and purple, like the passion that is hidden in every detail of my painting.

«One is here to teach. I'm learning all the time».
Mitsuharu Tsumura. MAIDO

THE OKONOMIYAKIS AND THE KITCHEN IN OSAKA

After five hours at the airport, I'm finally in my seat, trying to buckle up. I'm exhausted already, and the plane, which will take twenty hours to take me to my destination, has not even taken off yet. The best thing to do in these cases is to keep your mind busy to avoid thinking about your flying anxiety. I make sure that everything is in its place. The window is closed, the seat in the middle is unoccupied (because I bought both seats), no one is behind me, the suitcase is properly placed and everything I need is in my backpack. The headphones, the bottle of mineral water, my yellow pen and my notebook of invented recipes. Everything is under control.

It's been five years since I started my cooking studies, and there are still some pages left in this notebook that looks like it's about to explode; maybe this flight is a good opportunity to finish it and impress my grandfather. He doesn't understand anything about mixtures and fusions, but I'm sure I can convince him that a new form of life can be created in the kitchen, regardless of its origin.

Whenever I decide to keep myself busy, I end up getting distracted by something insignificant, but this time my eyes are too heavy. I don't even hear the flight attendant's voice giving the safety instructions. Wow, these pills seem to work well ...

I foreign languages; they guide me like a seeing-eye dog because my eyes still don't want to open. My body feels exhausted from the journey, but my other senses are more alert than ever. I can hear the hustle and bustle of people working and the smell of fish, as if I am in a seaport. The noise of trucks and giant cranes. The sharpening of knives. It's incredible that I haven't bumped into anyone yet, considering I can't see. My legs are carrying me to a roofed place that is completely silent. Actually, it seems that there is no one in the room, but I can hear the sound of the Sakai knives again; it is like a dance orchestrated with unique precision. Again, the smell of fish and seafood, but this time combined with other more sophisticated aromas, as if I am in a kitchen. A smell of chopped cabbage, flour, egg and dashi. Of seaweed, octopus, pickled ginger and spring onions. My mind mixes all the ingredients in a second and my mouth begins to water, imagining some tayokais and okonomiyakis.

The kitchen never misleads. I am in Osaka and, in the background, my grandfather is waiting for me with a uniform in his hand, pointing at the pile of dirty dishes that need to be cleaned. It's going to be a tough stay, but my stomach is impatient to taste everything that that kitchen has to teach me. It is so impatient that it starts roaring just when the plane is about to land.

THE HORSE MEAT AND HER

The sound of her keys at the door indicates the end of her shift. She is tired but happy because she is doing what she loves. Besides, tomorrow is one of those days when the stars align and we both have the same day off. She doesn't even turn on the light, but I can imagine the dark circles under her eyes and her wild, uncombed hair after taking off the gown she wears as a uniform.

When she enters the bedroom, she is already barefoot, having hardly any clothes on. She is holding a glass of sparkling water, drinking it in small sips, and when she leaves it on the dresser, she literally throws herself at me, forcing me to leave on the bedside table the book I had just started two minutes ago. She smiles and then kisses me. And so, lying on my chest while my fingers play with her hair, we begin the same conversation that precedes our only day off this week.

"Have you thought about what we're going to do tomorrow?"
"Day at home or lunch out?"
"Um... I don't know. What's in the fridge?"
"Well, let's see... ten bottles of sparkling water, a bottle of champagne, chili, leftover roast chicken and some horse meat. Oh! And your beauty cosmetics."
"Ha-ha, how funny! One of my creams is worth more than everything in the fridge."
"I know, I know. But you don't need those creams, honey."
"Don't be so smarmy, come on. It seems that we don't have many options. Maybe some rice with leftovers chicken? You know I don't like horse meat."

131

"What if we go to that restaurant that just opened? That way we can see how prepared their kitchen is."

"Their kitchen? You're always thinking about work, even on our day off ... Okay, you win, but we'll have breakfast in bed. I'm going to take a shower."

And so, she disappears behind a waterfall of hot water and steam. I think that I could live in this world only on horse meat, with her as my eternal dessert.

«Desserts are like mistresses. They are bad for you. So, if you are having one, you might as well have two».
Alain Ducasse. ALAIN DUCASSE

ADRIEN'S FIRST RATATOUILLE

I have a very special relationship with my grandson Adrien, perhaps because he gives me the opportunity to experience things that I couldn't with my own children. No matter how many trips I have to make or how busy I am, every week I find time for us.

Some time ago he and I made a gentleman's agreement. Adrien is only four years old, but he is like a miniature version of his grandfather, as shy, stubborn and creative as I am. Our deal is that, every day I spend with him in the playroom, he will learn the name of a new vegetable, we will pick it from the garden, prepare it in the kitchen and eat it together. In return, he decides what we will play that day, and his mother, by the way, is happy with this "vegetable game".

Whenever I arrive, Adrien already has a stage thoroughly set up in the living room and some made-up adventure that he tells me about while I admire his ability to create these universes from nothing. One day, he set up a castle where the king had thrown a banquet with many guests, but they had forgotten to prepare the food, so the adventure was to get Superchef to cook magical dishes in record time. Meanwhile his sidekick killed the dragon that wanted to ruin the party. Another day, he created a new planet where several astronauts were arriving for the first time, but one of them had lost the food and the mission was to look for something to eat on that deserted planet in order to survive. On that occasion, he even let me add some things to the story, so we ended up creating the first restaurant outside of planet Earth. Sometimes, I don't know which one of us is more childish.

Yesterday, I managed to leave the office early and I was looking forward to visiting my grandson, since today I have to travel again and I won't be able to see him for ten days. When I entered the playroom, I found him finishing a model plane full of cooks who had to rescue their chef from the clutches of Gros, the sorcerer. There was also a white forest, since it was snowing. Suddenly, my mind traveled to a past when my body could not move, but my mind worked 24 hours a day inventing new recipes, like the stories that my grandson creates.

I don't know how long I was lost in those memories. It surely wasn't long, since Adrien appeared with an old pilot's helmet, showing me how to fly the plane. This time he would be the chief pilot and I would be his assistant.

Afterwards, Adrien tried a ratatouille for the first time, and it was the first time that I allowed myself to think about the accident.

«We need to realize that we can only eat delicious foods if the natural environment is fine».
Yoshihiro. NARISAWA

THE SOUP RITUAL

Whenever we have an argument, I end up getting my stuff and leaving the house. It has become a ritual for us. He talks for minutes about his point of view or his feelings, rationalizing every sentence. I try not to interrupt him. I listen to him and then tell him that I don't think I can freely express my point of view without hurting him. That's when I leave. I do it quietly, without slamming doors or shouting, so I really don't know if we can call it an argument.

After leaving, I always go to the same place, the park near my house. Nature helps me relax and think clearly, and now that the cherry trees are blossoming, it is a pleasure for the senses. It's not easy to adapt to a new lifestyle when social customs are so different from yours. Here no one shouts, no one gets upset, everything is in order. And I look like a crazy person who gets upset about everything.

These walks always bring back memories of everything I have experienced in the last few years since I landed on this faraway island because of love. We are different in some ways, but I have always had a very chameleon-like personality, so here I am, still learning how to handle my arguments in a Zen way.

The walk lasts approximately less than two hours, enough time for me to almost forget why I left and for him to almost finish his part of the ritual.

When I head back home, I am always absentminded. A flood of thoughts about the beauty of the cherry trees, the sound of the ponds and the peace that can be breathed in this micro-world. This all in direct opposition to the noise and neon lights that overwhelm a city full of contrasts.

By the time I put the keys in the door, the house already smells of bonito and cedar, and it is heated by the steam coming out of the kitchen. I take off my shoes and finish setting the table. He approaches to kiss me on the cheek, a big step for him, who was not used to any kind of physical contact. Then, he gives me a taste of the soup he is preparing.

Perfect, as always. His soup tastes like a beautiful landscape, and that marks the end of our argument.

«I'd rather look for a long-forgotten vegetable or fruit than a new technique or some physical or chemical concoction».
Enrico Crippa. PIAZZA DUOMO

SALAD NUMBER 11

I am finally in bed, at exactly eleven o'clock at night. It seems that, until I close my eyes, the number eleven is going to keep chasing me.

This morning the alarm didn't go off and, although it's Sunday. I woke up in a bad mood when I saw that it was exactly 11:11. I'd lost most of the morning. When I took a shower, the thermostat had broken and was only setting the water at 11 degrees. I almost froze in the shower, but at least I was ready for brunch. While I was preparing it, I remembered the meals I used to eat in Japan, full of hot soups and rice. I really liked that dish of eels and rice that I tried somewhere between Tokyo and Kobe.

The microwave didn't want to heat the milk either, since only the number one option, which thaws for one minute, was working, so I ended up drinking my coffee black, deciding if it was too cold to go for a walk in the countryside.

In the end, I dared to leave the house. Well wrapped up, though. A breath of fresh air always helps me clear my mind from the hustle and bustle of work, and who knows if, with a little luck, I might find a hidden white truffle.

Well, I didn't find the truffle, but while I was fighting with the MP3 to stop it from playing the 11th song on the list on repeat. I came across a fallen nest, with 11 baby birds. I looked for some worms to feed them and then put the nest as high as I could on a branch.

With the good deed of the day, I hoped that the number 11 would stop chasing me, since it was already getting on my nerves.

After clearing my mind and stretching my legs, I decided to go to the restaurant before returning home. We were going to open it in 11 weeks and we still didn't know how to organize the distribution of the tables. I wanted small separate islands with different atmospheres, as though you could be eating in different places depending on your location. But my partner was more practical and wanted traditional tables. He was willing to give up two halls at most, with two different decorations.

He was there when I arrived, setting up tables in different positions and calculating the number of chairs. There were boxes scattered all over the floor, and one of them had an 11-piece dinner service, broken into pieces. He looked exhausted and, judging by his unfriendly face, hungry. Without telling him, I went to prepare a salad in the new kitchen, with 11 ingredients on the counter. We both needed to open the restaurant now, leaving behind the blueprints and numbers of a project that was making our lives miserable.

While we ate the salad in silence, I found the solution that would put an end to our problem. We would have 11 tables, which would be like eating at 11 different restaurants.

Maybe that's why the number 11 had been chasing me all day, to show me the solution that was in front of me all this time. Or maybe it's just the tiredness that made me see things where there weren't any. Maybe I should play the lottery and bet on the number 11.

*«We've always believed that the simplest food demands the
highest level of culinary skill».*
Kwok Keung Tung. THE CHAIRMAN

THE SECRET CRAB

At some point, things started to get difficult for those working in the service sector. Nothing pleased the customers; they were never satisfied, always leaving a bad review of the business they went to. Eventually, they would return the clothes they'd bought in stores, they would cancel their contracts with the telecommunications companies, and, in the restaurants, they would drive the cooks crazy by asking for changes to their dishes.

Long gone were the days when everyone followed the trends set by the media and social networks. Now everyone wanted to feel unique and special, and seeing someone wearing the same outfit as you was social suicide.

In the midst of this madness, Yin had a small restaurant located in a humble neighborhood in Hong Kong. At first, she wanted to please all her diners, so she tried to follow this trend of exclusivity and Aristotle's complex by inventing a digital menu in which every dish that was ordered disappeared from the menu. This way, each person knew that the dish they were eating was only for them and no one else could taste it that night. It was a success until people started demanding that each dish had to be served only once in a lifetime. Yin accepted the challenge, creating new dishes every day for months.

Her fame skyrocketed, but Yin became a slave to her diners, who only wanted to feel unique in the universe. One day, she found the solution to her problem; she decided to change the structure of the restaurant, creating small rooms where only two people could eat at each table. These rooms were like cubicles, with no view of any other part of the room. When someone arrived, the chef herself would welcome them in a small ceremony, asking them for their phones and cameras and placing them in a locker until their departure. Then, she would accompany them to their cubicle, where they would have to sign a confidentiality contract, stating that they could not reveal to anyone what dish they had eaten. This ceremony made them feel special, and everyone felt like someone important eating a secret dish, which they couldn't choose, since it was selected every night by the chef exclusively for them. Blinded by such pageantry, no one ever knew that the chef prepared the same dish for all of them: Crab noodles.

Yin had regained her freedom, and her diners always left with a smile on their faces.

«I remember the first time I entered a professional kitchen; my heart started to beat faster and faster. At that moment, I completely understood that I wanted to do this for the rest of my life».
José Avilez. BELCANTO

THE PORTUGUESE TEMPURA

I have always been fascinated by the things one can remember from one's own dreams, especially when they are things from "ancient" times. I always remember flavors, and everyone knows that there are flavors that take us back to our childhood. They stick extra hard to our brains because they are memories filled with the most unconditional love. Like the love I felt for my grandfather Ramón.

When I tasted the *pastel de nata* that Elvira brought me this morning, a chain of flavors and images invaded my mind. Although, none of them had to do with the pastry, but with fragments of the dreams I had the night before.

After the first bite, my palate was filled with tavern wine, salted almonds and olives. Those flavors came with the memory of the sea breeze that refreshed every summer morning, of my fast breathing chasing a ball that always went downhill, and of my grandfather's whistling while he played dominoes with his friends.

At that time, when I grew bored of playing the ball, I always ended up sitting on a step, half listening to the conversations of my grandfather with his pals and those of my grandmother with my mother in the kitchen. It was like a pendulum of sounds that went from the neighborhood gossip to the results of the local soccer team, from the recipes they had invented together to heated arguments over any topic.

I immediately remembered that morning when my grandfather claimed indignantly to his friends that it was us, the Portuguese, who taught the Japanese how to fry, no matter how famous their fried food might be, and that history had always stolen the spotlight from us. My grandfather was a Portuguese man, very proud of his land, always telling me a thousand stories about its kings, sailors and artists. On every occasion, he would advise me the same thing: "Don't allow them to make you believe that you are worth less than them."

In the background, my grandmother was preparing some eggs with mushrooms, and the memory of the spoon beating them brought me back to my kitchen, forty years later, where I am sitting with a notebook full of bland ideas. It's funny how your dreams can give you the inspiration you were looking for after spending hours in front of an empty plate.

«Reminiscing on our childhood years helps us present our dishes in a different and contemporary way».
Thomas and Mathias Sühring. SÜHRING

DUCK FEATHERS

I have a twin sister with whom for many years I only shared the same physique, except for the color of the eyes and a palindrome name. Both of us are five foot six, dark skinned like coffee, with curly brown hair and the same tiny freckles on the same parts of the body. But there are asmany differences. Her eyes are green and mine are blue. She loves science and I love literature. She is a vegetarian and I am more carnivorous than a cannibal. She loves mountains and I love beaches. And I could keep going until the end of time, because we were the most different twins in the world. And I say "were" because everything changed when we discovered Grandma's secret.

Amma and I hadn't seen each other for five years, and only an event as unfortunate as our grandmother's death could bring us together again. Funerals are not my thing, but my sister seems so composed that you feel like hugging her forever. Once we held a vigil for our Grandma and cremated her, our mother asked us to clean up the house, because it was too painful for her. And by "cleaning up the house" she meant putting everything in boxes, trying to get rid of as much as possible.

Amma has always been an ace when it comes to sorting things out; she's so meticulous that the CIA is missing out on a great talent. I think that, in another life, she was Japanese. You have to see how she folds the clothes, damn it. Truth is, I wasn't going to do much there, but I went with my sister to catch up. While she was assembling the boxes and taking everything out of the closets, I decided to open the drawers and rummage through them like I did when I was little. I know, that was of little help, but there are habits that never go away.

In one of the drawers I found a purple notebook, with a cover made from duck feathers, with all the pages yellowed and written with a handwriting that I recognized at once. It was some kind of recipe book, with many notes like a diary, as if they were pieces of advice or warnings, preceding each of the recipes. Without saying anything to Amma, I started reading the first page: "All cookbooks are the same, so if I have to spend all day in here, I'll make it fun. I'm going to try a new food every day, I'm going to take a bite and taste it. In doing so, I feel something that reminds me of a story, which leads me to create a new recipe..." I closed the recipe book at once and went out to find Amma, who was absorbed in her masterful organization.

I took her headphones off and showed her the notebook, pointing out what I had just read. She looked at me and we both knew what it meant. The two of us, who had never had anything in common, discovered at that moment that we had inherited that gift from our grandmother: The ability to imagine stories through a flavor, creating dishes that told those stories. After so many years, that purple book revealed what united us as twins, and we both decided to keep it a secret.

THE FIRST FISH

In the beginning of time, *A* created azure skies like a blue quandong and warm earth like a stew.

The dry land was chaotic and timid, so it grew inward until someone could find its secrets to awaken it. *A* realized that, under such darkness, the earth would never grow, so *A* said, "Let there be light," and light was created.

So, in order to prevent the earth from feeling lonely, *A* thought of other more adventurous universes that could give life to the earth when necessary. Then, *A* said, "Let there be the sea, wild and playful, the water of the rivers and the rain of the skies." And that's where the waves found a place to play with the winds and tides.

When the earth became wet, the seeds and trees with fruit appeared. So, in order to let the seeds know when to sprout, *A* kneaded the sun, the moon and the stars, which indicated the changes of season. Thus, each seed chose a different moment to emerge from the earth and see the light.

As a painter looking at his canvas, *A* felt that something was missing, so he molded the birds in the skies, the fish in the sea and all kinds of animals on the earth. With this natural mold, *A* kept painting flavors that gave life and color to the new world.

For a while, peace reigned in the world created by *A*. However, it was so perfect that it seemed dull to him, and it was then when he thought of inventing a couple of beings that would introduce new wisdom to that ideal world.

As A did not have many references, he created them using scraps of the wonders he had already invented. And so, from the earth and water, the two new beings had salt from the sea in their tongues and seeds from the trees in their hair. They had feathers on their arms and fur on their legs, so that they would not feel alienated from the world to which they had just arrived. A gave them his most precious power: his tongue. That way they would be able to recognize all the flavors he had created.

The two beings took some time to get used to the unknown, and every time they experienced something, they ended up creating a new invention. When they felt cold, they created clothes with the skins of beasts. When they felt hunger, they ate the fruits that the trees gave them. When they got bored, they invented new activities, like painting on stones. And then, one day, B, playing with some rocks, discovered fire. C, who had caught some fish, wondered what would happen if the fish were thrown into the red light that B had just discovered.

The first fish were carbonized, but the first cooks on earth had just been born. They would feed everyone and only care about the stars shining in the sky.

ACKNOWLEDGMENTS

I can't promise that I will be brief because this is my first book and I don't want to leave anyone out. As the saying goes, gratitude is the sign of noble souls.

To my blood family and in-laws, for being the number one fans of my stories. For encouraging me to write when I was a child by paying 100 pesetas for my poems. For keeping what I wrote as a child in a drawer. For putting up with how tiresome I can be, and for believing that this was possible even before I did.

To Gerard, for being with me 24/7 during the last stage of the writing process (the isolation virus caught us), and for always encouraging me to continue, no matter what setbacks may occur.

To my classmates at Colegio La Inmaculada, for their dedication during the crowdfunding stage, even though I haven't seen most of them in more than a decade. You are the best.

To my beta readers, for giving me your honest opinion and being the first ones to read this book.

To all the people who have collaborated and shared in their social networks the campaign to raise the money needed to make this dream come true, especially to Gema, who became my campaign manager and convinced the mayor of our town to get involved.

To Ana Jarén, for her magnificent work with the book cover. You are a wonderful artist.

To Sergio, for making the best book trailer in the world.

To my godson Anselmo, who was born just as I started writing these stories, giving me a good reason to stay grounded.

To you, for having read all these stories. For having this book in your hands. For letting me come into your life through this world of flavors and memories.

And to all those patrons who participated in Verkami's crowdfunding campaign, for being the first ones to believe in *Aperitales*. I hope it was worth the wait.

1. Cristina Vaquero
2. Verónica Freda
3. Pilar Ruiz Costa
4. María Dolores Marcos Armogienes
5. Coral Sol
6. Amy Din
7. María Carmen Jiménez
8. Pilar Díaz

9. Antonio Luis Alonso Zamora
10. Inmaculada García Gázquez
11. Xavi Hermoso
12. Ayumi Naito
13. Jerónimo Marcos García Gázquez
14. Diana Serrano
15. Lorena
16. Irene Gil
17. Gema García (the campaign manager)
18. Cristina Cote del Río
19. Irene López Bautista
20. Javier Puche
21. Carolina Ríos Gálvez
22. Guille Ocaña
23. Sonia Gutiérrez
24. M. J. Tello
25. Connie
26. Martin
27. Laly Codorniu
28. Asun Fernández
29. Natasha Zlobec
30. Jerónimo García
31. Nacho
32. Denise Carrillo
33. Mónica D. F.
34. Arantxa Esparza
35. Vanesa Cenizo
36. Ana B. Peñalosa
37. Verónica Santos
38. Desiré Gómez
39. Noe T. L.
40. Mercedes Rodríguez-Rubio
41. Gerard Puxhe
42. Cristina

43. Susana Caviedes Porteros
44. María Inés Criado

AUTHOR

Alba García Marcos (Algeciras, 1985) is a journalist who always has been linked to the world of communication and letters. She has lived in London since 2014.

On her blog, Las letras de Alba, she writes about fiction books and short stories in Spanish.

Apericuentos is her first book.

AUTHOR´S NOTES

Thanks for reading this book. I would love to hear your opinion through a review on Amazon. If you liked it, it would be great if you can recommend it to your friends and family.

Printed in Great Britain
by Amazon